I0638208

# Canyon Game

a novel
by

*Robert C.A. Goff*

**Dreamsplice**
Christiansburg, Virginia

This book is a work of fiction.

.

**Canyon Game**
a novel by Robert C.A. Goff

Copyright ©2025 by Dreamsplice

All rights reserved, including the right to reproduce this book, or
portions thereof, in any form.

Dreamsplice
3462 Dairy Road
Christiansburg, VA 24073

www.dreamsplice.com

Cover design by Robert C.A. Goff, Copyright © 2025 by Dreamsplice

ISBN-13: 979-8-9867728-6-8
Library of Congress Control Number: 2025908370
First Edition: June 2025

To my mother, Frances Earlene Roberts Amato Goff, who made my world possible.

RCAG

## About this book

For over three decades, I have been hesitant to publish this book. I felt it needed to be rewritten, but never found the motivation to do that. It was my very first attempt at a novel, written over a six week period in the autumn of 1992. It was the only completed novel that my mother lived to see.

I finally decided that I should publish it as is—warts and all. I had originally formatted it with a suitable, topographical map at the head of each chapter. I've since decided to omit the maps. Through the course of reformatting the manuscript into this book format, my incurable, editor's brain ended up with a re-write.

RCAG

## TUSAYAN

Staff Sergeant Jeffrey Horn struggled to make sense of the muddled sensations swirling about his mind. His eyes felt too big. No, he thought, my eyelids are too big. His head seemed to need more room inside to hold everything. His hips throbbed. The act of breathing had never seemed to require quite so much effort as now. *It's amazing how you breathe all your life, non stop, and never notice how much work it is.* He considered the possibility of being asleep, but rejected that on the basis of the persistent pain in his hips and in the front of his thighs. *Upside down. I'm upside down. Hanging from my hips. Hanging upside down.*

As his eyes crept open, he became aware of red, brilliant red. Red and white. The stained glass of a cathedral window to his left gradually resolved into the fracture patterns of a car window. Crystal and white and red. *Stained glass.*

Jeffrey Horn ached all over. He tilted his head upward and studied red-colored arms dangling toward a pool of red. *Blood. Blood and brain. Pieces of brain.* With effort, he drew his arms toward the top of his head, ignoring the cold and bruising from handcuffs about his wrists. His hands gently inspected the bald surface of the top of his head, then passed over sticky, bristling hair along the sides. *Not my brains.* He touched his face. No cuts.

Horn tilted his head once more to the mess on the inside roof of the car. "Christ!" The dreamy fog was clearing. His hoarse whisper amplified the surrounding silence.

Jeffrey Horn recalled the red veins in his father's eyes as the scratchy man told him that his mother had died in a car crash. Told him in gusts of beer breath. Told him those ordinary words with red veins in his eyes. He was three years old when she died. Perhaps her final moments were like this. He had wondered, over the years, if she knew she was about to die, or if she just plain died. Had she thought of him in that final moment?   Had she whispered, "Where is my J-J?" before she died?   Did she have time to think, like this?   He would never know.

But he was not dying.   He shook his head to clear his thoughts, then immediately regretted having disturbed his engorged brain.   By bracing his feet against the cage separating the rear seat from the front, he freed himself from the seat belt and lowered his body into the muck on the roof liner.   The rear door on the driver's side would not open.   A quick look at the opposite side indicated that both the door and window were firmly up against a snow covered embankment.        Returning to the window of the first door, Horn studied its fractures, then kicked at the glass.   It held.   He examined the cage frame, and realized that it offered no hope of an exit.   It was blocked in front by a wooden beam that had come from God knows where.   He turned and kicked at the glass with both feet.   As the glass gave way, Horn savored the rush of cold air on his ankles.   He extended his shackled hands through the window, and reached up to the door handle.   With a grunt, he leveraged his body past the flaps of broken safety glass.   Snow scooping into the collar of his coat and down his back jolted him fully into the present.

He sidestepped through the snow along the overturned car, which was buried up to the hood.   The upside-down shield painted on the driver's door read "County Sheriff".   The name of the county lay beneath the snow.   It didn't matter.   Not now.   What did matter was the handcuffs.

SSgt. Horn stooped by the driver's door and scraped away the crusted snow to reveal a few inches of empty window opening.   With growing optimism, he dug further and looked inside.   "Coconino County Sheriff".   The patch on the driver's shoulder had held his attention earlier this afternoon, when he was stopped for speeding on this icy, empty highway north of Flagstaff, then arrested for driving a stolen car.   Now, in place of the deputy's head, rested a scenic "Kaibab National Forest" sign, constructed of six-inch thick framing.   Horn surmised that it must have been sheared from its roadside posts, plunged through the windshield, and driven home when the squad car overturned in the gully and skidded on its roof.

With his cuffed hands, he reached through the narrow opening above the sign, fumbled under the deputy's jacket, and found the left shirt pocket.   Working only by the touch of his chilled fingertips, he searched for a key. He felt a pen, but no key. He tugged the shirt toward him and felt the right pocket. There it was, resting against the buttoned pocket flap. He knew that if he unbuttoned the pocket, he might lose the key.

Carefully, Horn inserted his index finger beneath the pocket flap, only to hear the ominous clink of metal striking wood. The key should be on the sign, he thought. His cold fingers glided slowly along the surface of the sign. A fingertip momentarily touched a small metal object, then it was gone. "Damn!" He removed the pen from the other pocket, withdrew his hands from the freezing puddle of blood above the sign, and stood to allow circulation to return to his feet.

Once again he stooped, and looked inside. The shotgun on the far side of the dash appeared to be crushed. He could see the glint of a plain gold wedding band on the dead man's left hand, and briefly wondered if the deputy had any children. They would hear about their father's death as he had heard of his mother's. He looked further. The grip of the deputy's service revolver was visible in the dim, red-stained light. His shackled hands groped toward the weapon and touched the tip of the butt. But, no matter how much he strained against the opening, he could not grasp the gun. The space between the door frame and the sign was too narrow.

*No weapon, and no key for the handcuffs.* Horn sighed, then nodded to himself. A day that could have ended behind bars, or on a marble slab, had instead turned out rather well. Attitude, he recalled. Attitude makes the difference between escape and capture.

The stream of Horn's thoughts drifted to a lecture he had presented fifteen months before, at Fairchild Air Force Base.

> *"If you don't believe in your own evasion skills, then you may as well give yourself up to the enemy and beg to be tortured." The wooden stage planking thuds beneath his slow pace as he lectures. "With a positive attitude, you may or may not get caught. With an attitude of failure, you will always fail. Isn't that right?"*
>
> *The audience, packed into the government-green lecture hall choruses, "Yes!"*
>
> *"This isn't just a game, is it?"*

*"No!" they respond loudly, with no more conviction than a high school pep rally.*

*The memory coalesces into an anguished face decorated with woodland tone camo makeup. It stares into Horn's eyes and shouts, "This is just a game!"*

Sparse, snow-covered conifers of northern Arizona returned. SSgt. Jeffrey Horn shivered in the cold of the December wind. He looked over his bloodstained denim jacket, grateful for the warmth of its fleece lining. He wished the jacket had been long enough to prevent the seatbelt from bruising his hips. He skillfully backtracked over the skid marks left by the car, pivoted on the blacktop and proudly scanned his path. No footprints. At the age of 28, he wasn't about to spend the rest of his life in prison for the death of a survival student. *It wasn't even my fault.* He walked south on the pavement 100 yards, painfully jumping over the patches of snow missed by the plow, except for the last narrow patch. Into that he planted one footprint, pointing south, then retrieved the deputy's bloody pen from his rear pocket and threw it as far south as he could, making certain that it landed on the pavement. He turned and headed north, again skipping over every area that might leave a footprint on the icy highway.

The exertion had driven away the cold, at least for the moment. After a twenty minute ritual of jogging, jumping, and turning to look back, he felt that this was truly a good day. The "Walking Air Force." He knew that the last two years as a survival instructor at Fairchild, not to mention the other six in the Air Force, had taught him all he needed to know at this juncture in his life. He knelt and carefully lifted a flat stone from the roadside, smoothing snow into the vacancy. Brushing the snow from the textbook-sized slab of limestone, he continued up the road, the cuffs abrading his wrists.

A speck appeared on the road, at the northern horizon, and seemed to grow in Horn's vision. *A car.* A glimmer of relief was immediately displaced by apprehension. He estimated that the car was still over a mile away. His heart and his pace quickened. Horn eyed a stony wash approaching within ten feet of the blacktop. Its seven foot northern wall was nearly vertical, striated with horizontal limestone. He pitched his stone halfway between the road surface and the ravine wall, landing it flat, without bouncing. A running start carried his right foot squarely onto the stepping stone, and his left foot onto a ledge of the wash. He gripped above to halt his motion, the cuffs digging painfully into his wrists, then hastily skimmed several handfuls of snow from the ravine bottom to dust the surface of the stepping stone. He was certain that only the closest inspection would reveal that he had passed this way. With his body pressed against the ravine wall, Horn watched as the car blurred past. Its markings were identical to the one from which he had just escaped. He was fairly sure that the driver had not seen him, but he knew that within two minutes, this car would reach the wreck. He side stepped east along the wash, his hands cold, bruised, and still shackled. His sense of victory was lost in the urgency of escape.

To Jeffrey Horn, the Kentucky Fried Chicken restaurant seemed like a better opportunity than the nearby McDonald's. He knew both should be closing soon. He wondered how either of them could make any money this time of year, with so few customers. But money was not his concern. It was food that he needed. After that, he thought, he could take care of the handcuffs.

For two nights he had traveled north through blowing snow, sleeping during the day. He had kept the highway barely visible to his left, confident that the wind and fresh snow would cover his tracks. He had not bothered to search for food. He knew that the desert in winter would offer him nothing.

Horn remembered a classmate in high school telling him that Kentucky Fried Chicken restaurants threw away any left over cooked chicken at the end of the day. He did not know if they still followed that rule. Besides, he thought, how much chicken would they cook this time of year, in this weather, in the little town of Tusayan? Maybe none. Or maybe the manager would take home the leftovers. Still, it seemed more promising to him than McDonald's, as he waited in the biting wind behind the rear parking lot.

The lights dimmed in the chicken restaurant. Aromas drifting from the two fast food establishments tore at his patience. Through a haze of snow gusting from the roof, he saw a rectangle of light appear in the rear of the building. A silhouette in a baseball cap emerged, hunched against the cold, carrying a partially filled bag to the dumpster. Horn waited until the figure returned to the building.      When he heard the door slam and the bolt clack, Horn sprinted across the parking lot to the dumpster. He lifted the plastic lid with his cuffed hands and peered inside at the jumble of plastic bags. The interior of the dumpster was illuminated by a security light behind McDonald's. After tossing the hinged lid over the dumpster, he identified two likely bags on top of the pile, and removed the nearest.      He placed it on the snow and hungrily tore it open with his bare hands.    The wind immediately sent three Styrofoam plates tumbling across the parking lot. He snatched up the first chicken bone and gnawed at the fleck of meat remaining at the joint. Frozen. This was the wrong bag. He threw the bag back into the dumpster and brought out the other of the partially filled bags from the top layer.

"What the hell are you doin' with that?" shouted a man's voice from behind him.

Startled, Horn spun around in his crouched position, lost his balance, and landed sitting in the snow with the unopened garbage bag in his lap. He stared up at the dark figure of a man whose face was obscured by the bright security light shining from behind. He seemed to hold a gun in his right hand. Horn's mind raced. He replayed in his mind the observations of the last few minutes. Nowhere could he find an explanation for a policeman or even an ordinary pedestrian appearing as this man had appeared.

"This is my place," the man said, with a hint of caution in his voice. He stepped to the side, keeping five feet of snow covered pavement between them.   Now Horn could see an unshaven old man standing before him in the blowing snow. The pungent odors of unbathed skin and whiskey reached Horn's nostrils as he recognized the shape in the man's hand to be a pint bottle wrapped in a paper bag.

Horn stood, held out the trash bag and said, "I'll split it with you."

The man backed away when Horn reached his full height. But when he saw the handcuffs, panic swept over his face. He turned and unsteadily ran four steps away from Horn before tripping over the curbing. Horn watched silently as the old man tumbled to the pavement, shattering his bottle, then hurriedly scrambled back to his feet to flee into the haze of blowing snow.

A wisp of pity and guilt touched Horn's consciousness for so brief a time that he perceived neither. The man ran into the darkness, rather than toward the main street, Horn thought with relief.

He turned his attention back to the garbage bag. Inside he found, above the dining litter, a separate, small bag containing three intact pieces of fried chicken, still warm. Horn suspected the manager was aware of the old man who came to dine at this dumpster. He returned the large bag to the dumpster and, starting with a huge mouthful, consumed the rest of the precious chicken as he walked the back alley toward Ned's Auto Repair, one block south. Along the way, he saw only one car pass on the main street, a block away.

The handcuffs, which not only abraded his wrists, but prevented him from putting his hands into his jacket pockets, needed to come off. Ned's Auto Repair, he was sure, would have something handy for cutting them. But the aging, single story cinder block building appeared well secured. He knew he shouldn't risk a front entrance. The side windows were guarded with well anchored iron bars, and the bulky rear door seemed to be bolted from the inside. The shadowed south side of the building offered one unprotected entry, a rectangular, one foot by two foot, horizontal window, seven feet from the ground. From its frosted glass pane, Horn assumed it led to a bathroom. Using a bent segment of rusted exhaust pipe, he knocked out the glass and attempted to remove the remaining glass shards from the frame. After waiting fifteen minutes in the back alley, to be certain that he had not triggered a silent alarm, he jumped up to the window, climbed through the narrow opening, and entered the darkened repair shop.

The light from the front windows was enough to enable him to recognize shadowy forms of tools on a workbench and on a pegboard above it. A well worn '78 Ford pickup stood on blocks, its engine resting on the floor nearby. With delight, he gathered a retractable shop knife, two pairs of vise-grip pliers, a hacksaw, and two files. He placed them into a black plastic trash bag. He decided that it would be smart to carry the tools and get well out of town before taking the time to remove the cuffs.

SSgt. Horn headed back toward the bathroom, but halted at the sight of an acetylene torch draped over a pair of gas tanks. The temptation to cut the cuffs in seconds rather than hours was more than he could resist.

Using a sparker, he lit the torch, adjusted the flame to a fine blue point, and in a magical three seconds, melted the center link of the cuffs. "Incredible!" He considered sawing the cuffs themselves in a safer place, but instead, gathered several rags, soaked them in water, then made a spackle of water and floor sweeping compound. The spackle he placed directly onto his skin between the left cuff and his wrist. The wet rags covered the neighboring skin. He braced himself for the pain, then cut the thinnest part of the cuff. During the last second, he felt the heat rapidly increase, but flung the cuff away without much pain. He repeated the process with the right cuff, but when he attempted to shake the hot metal away from his skin, the cuff remained on his wrist.

His body straightened involuntarily. He fell backwards, striking a rack of wooden shelves. Heavy objects rained down on his head and shoulders, then onto the floor. A wide mouth can struck the floor, bursting its lid and splashing liquid across the concrete toward the burning torch. In less than a second, a wall of flame erupted from the floor.

Jeffrey Horn stepped away from the flame, suppressing his panic with conscious effort. The hot cuff was gone from his right wrist, though he couldn't remember it falling off. The fire seemed to be spreading out in every direction. Another fallen can flared. He ran to the front door of the garage. He could see that it was key locked with a deadbolt. The overhead door looked as though he could open it, but that would be too conspicuous. With stinging eyes, he looked back into the flames. He fixed his gaze on the acetylene and oxygen tanks, which not only were near the fire, but were still open. He knew that he would die if he hesitated any longer. He ran, lungs aching, and jumped into the flames. His collision with the rear wall knocked the wind from his lungs. Panic was rising again. He staggered into the bathroom, stood on the sink, and slid out the window, landing painfully on his right side. Vaulting to his feet, Horn ran to the shadows and away from the garage as fast as his fatigued body would go. When he had traveled three blocks through the blowing snow, he heard the powerful explosion. This, he knew, would bring everyone out of their homes. He dropped into a copse of scrubby juniper.

During the hour that Horn huddled beneath the juniper, he watched the volunteer fire company dowse the shattered remains of the repair shop. The local spectators stood briefly in the falling snow, then returned to their homes. He casually walked north out of town in the snowy darkness.

## MATHER

David Cadranel frantically shifted both his thumbs over the controls of the Nintendo Game Boy. It was blaring its familiar "you're about to die" melody into his earphones. This really sucks, he thought, as he plopped the game onto his lap and tore away the earphones.

"It's about time, Davie. You've hogged it for the last two hours." Willie, who sat beside David in the cramped third seat of the GMC Suburban, reached for the Game Boy. David blocked Willie's arm with an instinctive parry. "God, Davie."

David, irritated with the game and with Willie, reluctantly tossed him the little box. For all his annoyance with the game, it had been his only respite from the overcrowding and inane conversations for the past two days of driving from Columbia, Missouri. To David, their entry into Grand Canyon National Park meant that this ordeal would finally end. For now, he suppressed his fears about what was to follow.

"Thanks, Davie," Willie mumbled, plugging his brain into the game, and instantly fading into the fantasy world of bleeps and liquid crystal people that David had just abandoned.

David Cadranel turned his head and looked briefly at Willie. He regretted coming. He had given in to Willie Thurman's insistence. This was originally planned as Willie's family vacation: Willie, his twin sister Laura and their parents. But he had learned over the years nothing was ever that straightforward when dealing with the Thurman family. He decided that fifteen years of raising the twins had given Mr. Thurman an odd approach to fairness and equality. At this particular moment, David had nothing but respect for Mrs. Thurman, since she had managed to avoid coming altogether.

David recalled the conversation two months ago that had led to his present predicament. Willie had come by the house with his algebra book in hand. Factoring polynomials had been Willie's latest devil.

*"So, what's the snag today, Willie?" David was not very fond of Willie. It wasn't that Willie was unpleasant. Willie was amiable enough. And it wasn't because he was ugly. Willie was every bit as pleasing to look at as Willie's twin sister, Laura. But Willie always seemed to want something or need something when he came by the house. David wasn't sure why he enjoyed helping him, but Willie's frequent visits were always more comfortable when a book was involved.*

*Willie stared at the closed algebra book in his hands, then set it beside him on David's neatly made bed. Loosely curled, light brown hair flopped over Willie's forehead. "I've got a major problem, Davie."*

*That was no surprise to David, since the miracle of Willie's B-minus average in most of his classes was due, in large part, to David's tutoring. Willie wasn't what David considered "dumb," but he seemed to lack the ability to work through things without a cheerleader egging him on. "Not Math?"*

*"Not math."*

*"Well?" David should have sensed the trap. Willie was never hesitant about asking him for help.*

*"It's my dad again."*

*"Another one of those famous hunting trips?"*

*"That's not funny. It's worse." Willie's braces flashed as he grimaced.*

*David was usually sympathetic when he heard about Mr. Thurman trying to goad Willie into one of his hunting trips. Willie played on David's soft spot.*

*"He wants me to hike the canyon this Christmas. Sort of a family trip."*

*David smiled. Mr. Thurman would have said, "It'll be a good trip." Meaning: maybe this will put hair on your chest.*

*"This time, Mom was on his side," Willie continued, "My sister took my side, if you can believe*

*that. She just doesn't want me to be there to spoil her trip. What a bitch."*

*"Are we talking about any old canyon, or The Canyon?"*

*"That's the one. The biggest mother of 'em all."*

*The silence gave David a distinct feeling that this had not ended with a simple, "No. I'm not going." on Willie's part. Willie didn't need a tutor; he needed a trainer or a coach.*

*"Have you ever seen the Grand Canyon, Davie?"*

*"Shit! This doesn't sound good. Why do I get the impression that I'm being dragged into this little family misunderstanding?" He tried to look straight into Willie's innocent blue eyes, but Willie was carefully tracing the letters ALGEBRA with his finger tip.*

*"You've gotta help, Davie. I said I would go if they let you come too."*

*"Not a chance." David hated hiking. Though he would never admit it to Willie, the thought of hiking the Canyon frightened him. He knew that people died there every year.*

*"Come on, Davie, you were a Scout."*

*"Great!" David removed the blue retainer from the roof of his mouth, then replaced it. "Three campouts in a state park. That'll work wonders in the Grand Canyon. I can barely pitch a tent. I can light a fire with a whole box of matches. And I can tie five knots. What more could you want? ...Oh, and if you want to cremate some hamburger and potatoes, I can show you how to fold the foil. Get real, Willie. I hate that shit as much as you do. I quit Scouts, remember? And besides, your father isn't exactly one of my biggest fans."*

*"He thinks you're okay, Davie. Dad's kind of...he...just doesn't know what to say to you, sometimes. Maybe you should shock him someday and show up at the house with a basketball or something."*

*"Your father would be happier, and definitely better off taking some brainless jock along instead of me," David replied. "Count me out."*

*"Then, I'll be stuck for nine miserable days. Nine days of my dad telling Laura how wonderful she is.*

*Nine days of my sister cackling with Alicia. Nine days of..."*

"Alicia?"

Willie hesitated. "Laura started bitching as soon as they said you could come. So Mom said Laura could ask Alicia."

"So you want me to blow away my Christmas vacation by spending the whole thing with your parents, your sister and her friend? Such a deal. A freshman's paradise."

"And Jay," Willie whispered, staring at the intricate designs in the small Baluchi rug beside David's bed.

"Oh, shit!" David walked over to the bed, knelt on the rug and twisted his head upside down until he could look up into his friend's inverted face: metal mouth on top, blue eyes below, and his light brown hair creating the image of a curly beard. "Earth to Willie. Do you read?" Exasperated, David went over and seated himself backwards on his armless swivel chair, and rolled to a position squarely in front of Willie. David's gangly legs extended to either side, with his size fifteen Nike's touching the bed frame. He pressed the question. "What's this about Jay?"

"Well, Dad got this crazy idea that if each of us got to invite somebody, then he and Mom should each get to invite somebody. Made sense to Dad, anyway."

"It would," David mumbled.

"Well, everybody Mom knows knits and makes quilts and apple pies for a hobby. So she told Dad to invite somebody, if he wanted to."

"And he picked another kid?"

"Not exactly. He asked one of his poker buddies, but he had to work."

"Jay's father?"

"Now you see why you have to go, Davie."

"No, Willie. With that asshole going, I have an even better reason not to go. The answer is a plain, ordinary, 'No!'"

That was two months ago.  Here he was now, massaging the cramps out of his legs from sitting in the shrunken third seat of the Suburban, with his bony knees near his chin.  Without the Game Boy, he found it difficult to ignore the incessant chatter between Alicia Waters, who sat in front of him, and Willie's twin sister, Laura, who knelt backwards in the bucket seat up front.

The mouths on these two fifteen year old girls represented the closest thing to true perpetual motion that David had ever witnessed.  He didn't expect to be included in their conversations.  Since they had hardly acknowledged his existence during the past two days, he had no reason to think the remaining seven days would be any different.

"Dammit," mumbled Jay Vesco, who was also immersed in the electronic seclusion of a Game Boy.

"Getting your butt kicked?" David asked, loudly enough to penetrate Jay's earphones.

Jay paused his game, turned his head slowly to David and whispered, "Fuck off, faggot," then returned to his game.

Jay sat behind Mr. Thurman.  The center seat next to Jay remained empty.  Ever since Jay had staked claim to his seat at the start of the trip, David observed that no one would take the adjoining seat.  He knew why he avoided it.  He detested Jay Vesco.  As for everyone else's reasons, he wasn't sure.  David acknowledged that Jay was unquestionably the most popular boy in the freshman class at the high school.  He was the quarterback for their championship JV football team.  At school, David would watch in amazement as the girls fell over themselves to date Jay.  David had heard from reliable sources that Jay had scored with a dozen girls in just the past four months.  He also knew that Jay and Laura had been pretty serious at one time.  But Laura now sat the farthest from Jay.

Looking past Willie, David could see a rocky, snow covered roadside dotted with twisted juniper, sparse stands of pinyon and an occasional Ponderosa pine.  He knew that the Grand Canyon was off to the right, mostly shrouded in low clouds, but there wasn't much of a view from the car.  Besides, he thought, he'd seen it all in pictures.

"Radio says they're tracking a runaway killer around here," Mr. Thurman said calmly to his daughter.

"Here at the canyon?" Alicia shouted up to Mr. Thurman.

"Yes," Mr. Thurman bellowed at the rear view mirror.

"They said he escaped somewhere north of Flagstaff and might be headed toward the Canyon, but they're not sure."

David became aware of the din of the radio up front. With Mr. Thurman at the radio controls, the rear speakers had been turned off only fifty miles out of Columbia as one of the terms of a radio peace treaty.

"Who are you talking about?"    David directed the question at Alicia.

Laura Thurman, who had righted herself to listen to the radio, spun back around to answer.  "An Air Force guy wanted for murder in Washington State. He might be headed toward the Canyon. That's really creepy."

"They say there's supposed to be another severe winter storm headed this way." Mr. Thurman was lapsing into his play-by-play radio commentary again.  Middle age men, David had decided, tended to think everybody wanted to hear the news and weather.

The interstate through the mountains of New Mexico had been buried in a fresh snowfall that morning.  It had been the trigger for Mr. Thurman's forty minute diatribe on the fools who try to drive winter highways in their underpowered city cars.

Laura leaned over the back of the seat and moved her head close to Alicia.  "Don't worry about the escaped killer; Jay will protect us."

Alicia looked over at the football player exercising his thumbs on the Game Boy.  "Yeah, right." She and Laura laughed.

"What?  What's so funny?" Jay asked, having caught their laughter and glances out of the corner of his eye.

"You wouldn't understand, Jay," said Laura, with a twinge of arrogance in her voice, "It's complicated."

Jay puckered his lips in a contemptuous kiss for each of the girls.

Laura rolled her eyes and whispered something to Alicia. They laughed again.

Jay ignored them and returned to his game.


In the fading light, Jeffrey Horn lifted the lid of yet another garbage dumpster.  He was tense.  He had seen too many sheriff's cars moving along the highway today.  As he searched the garbage, he kept an eye on the rear of the aging apartment building as well as the approaches to its parking lot. So far, he had found a block of slightly moldy cheddar in a plastic sandwich bag. Now he saw a full bag of scorched microwave popcorn.

A Park Service car slowly turned into the front parking lot. The ranger looked directly toward him. Horn was sure that he had been seen. The car was about forty yards from him. Don't run. With a broad smile, he waved to the ranger, closed the lid, leaving his food hidden behind the dumpster, then walked toward a door at the rear of the building. As soon as he was out of sight and onto the shoveled pavement, he ran to the far corner of the building and crouched beside a parked Toyota. The ranger's car cruised the snow covered drive between the building and the dumpsters, then continued through the lot and back to the road.

Way too close, Horn thought. He returned to the dumpster, picked up his cheddar and popcorn, then opened the same dumpster again to retrieve something that had caught his attention at the moment the Park Service car had forced him to hide. He pulled out an empty gallon size Clorox bottle.

*Excellent!* He was satisfied with himself as he hurried into the forest scrub.


The Suburban headed up the blacktop of Mather Campground, turning at the first open gate. In the fading light, David could see one empty site after another. Only two had vehicles parked on the pull-offs from the single lane pavement. Within minutes, David was wrestling with his tent.

"What if that killer sneaks into our campsite tonight?" Alicia asked Laura. They were struggling to push tent stakes into the frozen, rocky ground of the campsite.

"He'll probably kill all the guys," Jay interrupted, "then rape you and Laura."

"You're such an ass," Laura replied. "Why don't you give us some help, instead of reassurance?"

"Maybe I should sleep in your tent, just in case," he offered.

"In your dreams," Laura mumbled.

"Of course, maybe he's queer and he'll kill us and spend the night playing with the faggots," Jay added, gesturing toward David and Willie, who were setting up their own tent.

"You're disgusting," Alicia said simply.  She and Laura added the fly to the tent.

"Maybe he has a thing for black girls," Jay said to Alicia, emphasizing "black" with an affected southern accent.

David knew that Alicia resented the label "black."  His father had described her skin as a delicate cafe-au-lait.  David thought her skin more closely matched the golden-tan Spanish Claro wrappers of his father's favorite Honduran cigars.  Either way, she was easily the most beautiful girl that David had ever met.

"Or maybe he has a thing for ignorant rednecks," Alicia retorted.

"Oooh."  Jay retreated to the tent he shared with Mr. Thurman.

Laura bounced over to her father.  "Good night, Daddy," she said, hugging him.

"Ow, my neck is stiff," he complained.

"Here," Laura instructed, turning him around and firmly massaging his shoulders and neck.

"Mmm, that's wonderful, Sugar," he said, closing his eyes.

"That's upside down," Willie grumbled at David, indicating their tent fly.

"Well how the hell am I supposed to know which side goes up?" David snapped, realizing that he had been watching the others, instead of his tent.

"Aside from the big word 'Eureka' printed on it, and the snaps that only fit one way, I don't know," Willie said sarcastically.

Without another word, David turned the fly over and attached it. He couldn't believe that he had agreed to come with Willie. Seven more days of this shit. He unrolled his sleeping bag in the tent, undressed, and crawled into the bag, ignoring Willie, who was reciprocating the show of annoyance.

After fifteen minutes, Willie's breathing assumed a cadence of sleep.  Conversations trailed off in the other tents. David wondered if he would be able to fall asleep tomorrow, after a day of hiking.  When he had trouble falling asleep at home, he would put on his sweats and go down to the living room to read.

Here, in his sleeping bag, he felt toasty warm, and preferred to stay right where he was. But he could foresee staring at the nylon wall for at least another hour if he lay there. Being an only child made it difficult for him to fall asleep with someone else so close. He leaned over in the near-darkness and looked at Willie's face. Although Willie resembled his twin sister, he appeared about thirteen years old, instead of his actual fifteen years. Beneath the loose curls of hair, Willie's face was unblemished, whereas his own face always sported at least a zit or two.

David was puzzled by Willie's friendship. Willie seemed to like him, not caring that David's legs were too long, feet too big or that he was clumsy at every sport he attempted. Rather than ridiculing him for his high grades and love of books, Willie came to him often, to ask for help. David seldom trusted Willie with his secrets. Though they were the same age, David regarded Willie as a younger brother.

David unzipped his sleeping bag, dug through his pile of clothes, then pulled on his long johns and his size 15 camp slippers. He zipped up his fleece jacket, which served double duty as a pillow, then unzipped the door and went out into the still, December air of the Coconino Plateau. He guessed the temperature to be about twenty degrees. The wind was still.

About forty feet away, he saw the flare of a cigarette lighter briefly illuminate Mr. Thurman's face. The light disappeared, leaving a red, glowing dot. David breathed the Winter vapors of Northern Arizona. He could smell the pinyon and juniper, which dominated the rocky, snow-dusted campsite. He put his face against the three foot thick trunk of the nearby Ponderosa pine and sniffed its bark. There was a distinct, sweet aroma that reminded him of vanilla and of his mother's cheesecake. As the quarter moon cleared the trees, Mr. Thurman disappeared into his tent.

David swept his gaze around a full circle, wondering what might be hidden in the shadows beyond blue-white snow. Something moved beneath the trees thirty yards away. He stared in that direction for several minutes, then decided that his eyes must have tricked him. He returned to his tent and climbed directly into his sleeping bag. Starting at his feet, he removed his slippers, his long johns, and finally his fleece jacket, which he rolled up and placed beneath his head. The taffeta lining of the sleeping bag momentarily chilled his bare skin, raising goose bumps from his shoulders to his ankles. After fifteen seconds, his sleeping bag regained its cozy warmth.


Jeffrey Horn hid in the trees until the last camper had gone into his tent, then approached. The Suburban was locked, as was its rooftop carrier. He could see useful gear within the car. They had left nothing outside the tents except one walking stick. He walked over to a sagging tent set up beneath a huge Ponderosa pine and took the walking stick. It might be handy when he climbed into the Canyon.

   Horn went to the tent which he had seen the girls enter. Squatting near the fabric wall, he listened to the soft breathing and imagined its fairy touch against his shoulder.

## HERMIT

An overcast sky carried a hint of dawn when Jeffrey Horn awakened in the gravel pit that had been his bed for the night. He had decided to wait to climb into the Canyon in the daylight, afraid that the upper trails would be icy. With his stolen walking stick in his right hand and the salvaged Clorox bottle filled with water in the left, he headed west on a snow covered jeep trail.

He worried that the water in the bottle was beginning to freeze. By occasionally banging it against his leg, he found that he could prevent the surface from freezing over. Soon, he assumed, the warmer air within the Canyon would eliminate that problem. But as he had discovered while walking last night, the weight of the full bottle required him to trade hands every few minutes.

After a mile and a half, he approached Rim Drive. He skirted to the south of it until he reached the trail head marked Hermit Trail. There were two locked and apparently empty cars parked in the gravel lot. He saw no hikers or rangers. A moment of envy possessed him, as he considered how different this would be with the right equipment and supplies, and without people chasing him. The words echoed again within his mind, *"This is just a game!"* He stepped over the rim.

To his relief, the trail surface showed very little ice. He moved quickly down the switchbacks for half an hour, passing one trail junction that seemed to head back out of the Canyon.

At the second junction he stopped to study his options. The fork to the eastern slope was free of snow and ice, but the west fork, marked "Boucher Trail" on a wooden sign, led through the snow in the shaded head of the side canyon. The eastern fork would clearly be safer walking, but if he could leave tracks heading west, then he could lead his pursuers in that direction while he doubled back to the East in the snow-free trails below.

"How likely is that?" asked Ranger Maria Sanchez.

"Not very," was the glib reply from her boss. "Why would somebody with so much survival training be so careless that he'd walk into the world's biggest trap?"

Although Bill Gluzack was three years her junior, Maria Sanchez respected his more extensive knowledge and experience in law enforcement, however reluctantly. As a backcountry ranger, Sanchez knew that her only police experience had come before her twelve years in the National Park Service. Her three year stint as a paramedic with the San Antonio Police Department wasn't what she considered real police work. "So do we just wait?" she asked.

"Well, it's not like we have to worry about hordes of tourists and hikers right now," Gluzack replied.

In that, she knew Gluzack was right. The cascade of winter storms had succeeded in turning away the usual onrush of Christmas visitors to the Canyon. The number of casual tourists was practically nil, and the hikers and backpackers she had checked through in the past few days had been honed down to only the most obsessive.

"I just don't like the thought of having to manage hikers in the backcountry with a killer wandering..."

"First of all," Gluzack instructed, holding up his index finger, "Sergeant Horn isn't a killer; he's a suspect who just happens to be fleeing."

"That's a comfort." Maria Sanchez had become accustomed to hiding her annoyance at Gluzack's interruptions.

"And second, the County Sheriff doesn't know where he's headed."

Sanchez conceded that as Director of Backcountry Services, Ranger Gluzack resolved tactical decisions of this sort daily, gathering the divergent scraps of data and transforming them into a definitive decision.

"The ice and snow may force us to shut down," he continued, "but until the best information suggests that Horn is entering the Park, he's not part of the equation."

"Whatever you say, Bill." Maria Sanchez was still uncomfortable with the possibilities, but she wasn't sure if that was because of the facts involved, or because she basically distrusted quick decisions, especially when it was a man making the quick decision. "So what's the Weather Service saying today?"

Bill Gluzack scraped his wooden chair out from under him and strolled over to the fax machine that brought forecasts and weather maps to the Backcountry Reservations Office. She watched him shuffle through a nest of fax sheets and extract two pages. Tossing the rest back into the basket, he studied the selected reports as he walked.

"Looks like this one's going to miss us," he concluded.

"At least that's some good news." Sanchez stood and began to set up the paperwork. She would open the Backcountry Reservations Office, known to Canyon hikers as the BRO, in three minutes. Gluzack vanished into his back office.

Ranger Sanchez walked around the display boards in the hiker's waiting area and unlocked the front door. Instead of the usual cross-section of social strata, from the barely equipped to the proud wearers of Eddie Bauer's finest, she saw one party of six generic hikers standing on the BRO's front porch. The well plowed parking lot was nearly empty. A GMC Suburban with a large roof top carrier was parked near the office.

"Are you open?" asked the only adult in the group.

"As of right now. Come on in and warm up," said Ranger Sanchez, holding the door while they entered. "You're among the few and the brave these days."

"It's the only way," the middle aged man stated, with apparent sincerity. His solid build and slight paunch suggested to Sanchez that he was an active man, but not very well conditioned for backpacking on the brutal trails of the Canyon.

Sanchez moved to the office side of the desk area and looked through the three forms in today's basket. "Are you the Thurman party?" She looked up and saw four teenagers wandering among the rows of six foot high display boards that dominated the waiting area.

"That's the one. I'm Phil Thurman." He kept his hands in his jacket pockets.

"Laura Thurman," said a confident teenage girl, with a polite smile and the offer of a handshake.

"Maria Sanchez," the ranger replied, with a solid shake of Laura's hand.  She slid a copy of a densely typed sheet of regulations in front of Mr. Thurman.  "Please read these and sign here.  You'll need to make sure all the members of your party understand the rules and follow them."

Phil signed.  Laura read the rules.

"I hiked the Canyon last Christmas," Phil announced.

"Where did you hike?" asked Sanchez.

"All the way to the bottom and back."  Phil apparently assumed that was sufficiently impressive to establish his credentials.

"Down The Corridor?... The Bright Angel Trail?"

"Yeah, that's the one.  Quite a hike," he added proudly.

"That's a good introduction to the Canyon," Sanchez said diplomatically.  "I'm sure you'll find the Hermit loop... uh... more challenging."

"How do you mean?" Phil asked with a slight wrinkle to his brow.

"The Hermit trail hasn't been maintained by the Park Service for over sixty years.  Rock slides have buried parts of the trail, and you'll see that it's narrower and a little more exposed than the Bright Angel."

"That sounds kind of dangerous," Laura said, looking at Phil, whom Sanchez assumed was the girl's father.

Phil smiled.  "I'm sure it's safe."  He looked to Sanchez.  "Isn't it?"

"Well, there is a little less shoulder separating the trail from the fast way down.  But it's more of a visual impression.  There are no really dangerous stretches, as long as you stick with the trail," Sanchez clarified.  "Oh, there are two other things."

Sanchez noticed that the handsome, muscular boy had approached, and that he was conspicuously checking out her body with his unflinching eyes.  "You'll need instep crampons," she continued, "for the first 400 vertical feet.  The upper trails are covered with ice and crusted snow.  You don't want to be slipping and sliding up there.  And also be careful near the river, since Glen Canyon Dam has been increasing the amount of water they release."

"Do we have instep crampons, Daddy," Laura asked.

"We got 'em for everybody, Sugar.  They're those little toothed things that strap on the bottom of your boot."

"So we're going to be ice skating with backpacks on thousand foot cliffs?," Laura commented. "That's really good."

"Are you really a ranger?" the handsome boy asked Sanchez.

"No," she replied dead pan, "I only wear this uniform every day because I look so good in green. All of you have a safe hike." To Laura she added with a wink, "Don't let these hombres talk you into carrying any of their junk when they get tired."

Laura smiled. "Maybe for a small fee."

"Let's go, troops," called Phil Thurman to the restless teenagers standing by the map tables.

Maria Sanchez watched them leave. She felt a little younger than when she woke up this morning. The boy who had made the clumsy pass at her couldn't have been older than sixteen. She considered herself rugged, trim and superbly conditioned for a woman of thirty-seven. She knew that this was in part because she had served as a climbing ranger at Rocky Mountain National Park before coming to the Canyon, gaining the summit of Long's Peak three times—each by a different route. Now she spent most of her time hiking in the back country of the Grand Canyon. The endless paperwork aside, she knew this was a dream job, especially if it kept her in good enough shape to have a sixteen year old flatter her occasionally.

Sanchez walked into Gluzack's office. "Bill, you're comfortable about this Sergeant Horn thing?"

"Maria, if he went into the Canyon without supplies for a long stay, he'd have to come back out one of the trails to the South Rim. They're not too hard to watch. The North Rim is in five feet of new snow this morning. Phantom Ranch is staffed by five people right now, so just getting across the river to the north side would be chancy. It just wouldn't make sense."

"I guess." Maria Sanchez was not convinced.

"He taught survival school. An instructor."

"You're the boss," Sanchez reluctantly returned to the paperwork out front.


Jeffrey Horn stood motionless. To go forward along the sloped ice, he would have to accept death as a possible outcome. The trail had contoured north along the upper layers of the Canyon. It had seemed safe enough at first. Now the trail narrowed to the width of his shoulders. To the left, the rising wall appeared to lean toward the trail. To the right, the drop exceeded his imagination. No shoulder separated the trail from that certain death. Beneath his feet lay a crown of ice, smooth as a polished wood floor, and sloping toward the gaping maw. He wished he had crampons.

Turning around now would mean surrender. He had intentionally left tracks in the snow for his pursuers. Horn considered whether to surrender or risk death. It would be a quick death. He would fall three, maybe six seconds, then....

His numb fingers passed along the crumbling rock to his left. One hand was nearly useless with the Clorox bottle. He had stuffed the walking stick down the back of his denim jacket. He knew he would die in the Canyon without a water bottle. He leaned against the rock, opened the bottle, and filled his stomach with water. Horn faced the wall and continued his side step. The lighter bottle now hung by two fingers. His eyes shifted frantically between the wall and the trail as he moved. *The cap!* His fingers had been so numb that he had forgotten that he was holding it. He looked. The cap was gone. He resumed the terrifying traverse.

Horn saw the trail widen ten feet ahead. He inched along. His right foot lost its traction. A prickly sensation of horror surged through him. His chest struck the ice. Jeffrey Horn slid headlong toward the edge, coming to a stop face down, with his head and shoulders poised over the abyss. A wave of nausea swept over him. He could only close his eyes and wait. He counted silently to six, satisfied with how quickly death would have come.

After a minute, with his eyes still closed, he squirmed his way back onto the trail. He would belly crawl the remaining distance to the widening of the trail.


David Cadranel surveyed the nearly empty parking lot. The wooden sign said, "Hermit Trail Head." Mr. Thurman stood on the sill of the Suburban's open rear door. He lifted backpacking gear from the rooftop carrier and passed it down to Jay.

"The coach is gonna be impressed with your toughness when you get done here, Jay, my man," Mr. Thurman said. "Your legs'll be like iron."

"He'll be happy as long as I don't break my legs, Mr. T,"
Jay replied.

David knew that Jay Vesco had been in training for
football and basketball for six months. According to Willie, the
fifteen year old freshman had already received two under-the-
table inquires from university athletic departments. David was
also aware that the six foot one, 160 pound quarterback had
received dozens of inquiries from girls at his school.

David squatted over his backpack and yanked on its
vertical lashing straps to compact the load and prevent it from
shifting. He could never hope to have Jay's physique or his
popularity. He was grateful at least, to be less of a wimp than
Willie.

The seven mile drive from the BRO to the trail head at
Hermit's Rest had been a disappointment to David. He had
hoped to finally see some of the Canyon. The one stop at Hopi
Point had revealed only a cloud-filled trench under the clear
Arizona sky.

David hefted his thirty-three pound pack and adjusted
the padded hip belt to ride snugly over his 27-inch hips. As the
six of them approached the head of Hermit Trail, Jay threw a
palm sized shard of sandstone into the gaping, misty canyon.

"That's the farthest I'll ever throw a pass."

"That wasn't too smart, Jay," said David.

"What's the problem?" Jay asked, daring David to justify
his parental comment.

"The rock. It could fall two thousand feet before it lands."

"So?"

"It could kill somebody." David was now defensive.

"If I do kill somebody, you'll be the first to know. Besides,
who appointed you Mother?"

One by one they stepped onto Hermit Trail and below the
rim of the Canyon. As if on cue, David watched the clouds clear
from the Canyon, revealing the impossibly vast gouge into the
earth. Terraces stacked upon slopes balanced upon cliffs,
stacked upon still more terraces, were crowned with spires and
sunlit temples as far as he could see. David's mind could not
grasp what his eyes took in. He halted, breathless as his vision
absorbed the horizontal bands of color across the side canyons
and intricate drainages.

The Canyon geology he had forced himself to study had been only labels on a diagram. He silently named the strata splashed before him in hues of beige, tan, umber, rust, purple, gray-green and black. Nothing in his experience had prepared him for this stutter in the earth's crust. At the distant bottom he saw a jagged crack, the edge of which, he knew, was the top of the thousand foot deep, inner gorge. At its bottom, a mile below him, raged the Colorado River.

"Holy shit!" whispered Willie.

David realized that Willie had been standing just above him on the rock strewn trail. "I agree," David said. "Where's your walking stick?"

"I couldn't find it."

Willie and David allowed the others to pass out of sight beyond the first switchback. They continued down the broken path, occasionally seeing some of their companions moving below. After twenty minutes of strenuous, uninterrupted descent they caught up with the party taking their first rest break.

David walked toward the Alicia, who sat at the rear of the group, retying her bootlace. He realized that Alicia's backpack was tipping over. She had taken it off and braced it upright against a boulder on the canyon side of the trail.

"Alicia...," he yelled, trotting toward her as fast as his own backpack would allow.

Alicia's only response was to look at him in amazement. He saw the meaning finally dawn on Alicia. She turned her head in time to watch her new external frame backpack, with all her belongings, tumble over the edge.

"Oh, my Lord," she muttered.

No one moved, except David. In an attempt to slow himself before he followed Alicia's backpack over the brink, David tripped over his own feet. The full length of his lean body assumed a momentary hover, parallel to the rocky trail. Then he crashed, outstretched, onto the ground, with his palms at his shoulders to keep his face from planting itself into the remnants of flagstone paving. For an instant, David recognized that he wasn't seriously injured. But in that fraction of time, his own backpack ended its free-fall and slammed him into the ground for a second time.

David lifted his bruised chin from the stone and dirt. He became aware of Willie helping him up.

"Holy jeeze, are you okay, Davie?"

"Let me look." Someone was dusting the dirt from his bony knees, face and palms. "Do you hurt anywhere?"

David's thoughts were a little fuzzy, but he felt fine. The pack?

"You seem to be in one piece." It was Alicia.

David furrowed his brow and looked at the spot where Alicia's pack had vanished.

"That was impressive, Davie." Laura Thurman was behind him, speaking with sarcasm. "I hope you're not going to start charging admission."

"What happened to the pack?" he asked Willie. David fixed his eyes on the figure standing at the outside edge of the trail, then walked over.

Five hikers now stood shoulder to shoulder at the edge of the trail, looking down. David saw Jay Vesco scrambling fifty feet below, at the base of a series of ledges and scree slopes. On his back was Alicia's backpack. David was relieved to see that Alicia had not chosen to test fly her pack over one of the sheer cliffs visible in every direction, most offering a straight drop of up to six hundred feet.

"There's kind of a path to your left," David shouted.

Jay stopped, looked at David silently, then proceeded to his right.

"No, your left." David assumed that Jay had misunderstood his suggestion.

Jay continued in the opposite direction without acknowledging David a second time. David watched as Jay climbed, slid, and struggled his way back to the trail. With a victorious glare toward David, Jay handed the fairly intact backpack to Alicia by holding it in two fingers and extending his right arm.

"Thanks," Alicia mumbled, quickly turning away from Jay.

"No problem." Jay returned to his own pack, extracted a water bottle from an unzipped side pocket and quenched his thirst.

David followed his example, doffing his backpack, with a little help from Willie, and drinking from a water bottle. He kept a pint bottle in his fanny pack, worn to the front, but he saved that water for thirsty moments between the hourly rest breaks.

Mr. Thurman sat sculpting an empty oval of moleskin, his thick fingers barely able to fit the openings in the tiny folding scissors. He peeled the paper backing, flicked it onto the trail, and placed the pad of moleskin over a red welt near the base of his left big toe. "This stuff is a miracle." He pulled on his liner sock, the wool sock and his boot.

"I can't believe you didn't break something, Davie," said Willie, who sat beside David's pack. "You crashed like the coyote in the cartoons."

"It wasn't that big a deal, Willie."

"Right," Willie agreed, "You didn't leave a hole the shape of your body in the middle of the trail."

David sighed when the party strapped in and buckled up. With Willie and David being the slowest at this, they were again in the rear of the line, as the trek to Hermit Campground resumed. David considered Mr. Thurman's tiny scrap of litter as he passed. With a backpack, he thought, it's not worth it to bend over.

"We haven't seen any snow or ice on the trail yet," said Willie. "Maybe we'll see some further down."

"I think we lucked out," replied David. "We're starting into the Coconino, and we'll be too far down, pretty soon."

"The Coconino?"

"See that cream colored cliff over there?" David pointed his walking stick across the gorge of Hermit Creek to a three hundred foot cliff, high on the Canyon wall. "That's the Coconino, and were just about down to it."

"I thought you'd never even been here before, Davie."

Before setting foot in the Canyon, David Cadranel could draw from memory a map of the Hermit loop, which they were presently hiking, and could name the major strata of the Canyon, describing their unique colors and their erosion patterns, whether cliffs or slopes. The truth of the matter was that David felt safe with books. The reality of the Canyon staggered his mind.

"I read about it."

His understatement hid his fear. David had been so frightened by the prospect of hiking the Grand Canyon, that he had spent the last two months reading about the Canyon. He read while tracing his finger along the trails of maps. His father had helped him locate the best references. He had read everything from Colin Fletcher's beautiful narrative of his solo hike through the length of the Canyon, to the terse details of Harvey Butchart's tiny books.

Below the precipitous switchbacks of the Coconino, David and Willie trudged through the deep red slopes of Hermit Shale. Sixteen hundred vertical feet below the trail head, past the eroded inclines of rusted shale, he saw the rest house at Santa Maria Spring. It clung to a slope below the Esplanade, the red-brown sandstone cap of the Supai Formation. David recognized pinyon and juniper dotting the slopes that had formed over the eons from the disintegration of the surrounding cliffs. He looked above. Cream colored sandstone walls peeked through clefts in the jagged rock.

David and Willie again caught up with the others filling water bottles at a trough south of the rest house. Part of the flow of Santa Maria Spring trickled from a pipe. After drinking the remainder of one of his own bottles, David filled it, unzipped his fanny pack and opened a tiny bottle of water purification tablets. He dropped one tablet into the water bottle.

David leaned his backpack against the sparsely mortared sandstone wall of the rest house. He stepped into the open front, passing under an ivy vine so old that its stem had grown to a diameter of five inches, taking on the appearance of a dwarfed cottonwood tree. Inside, he dropped himself onto a wooden slab bench, polished, he guessed, by sixty years of equally weary hikers.

"God almighty, my feet hurt," Mr. Thurman groaned. He deposited himself in front of the rest house and unlaced a boot.

"How about a snack break, Daddy?" Laura asked.

"Good idea, Sugar," he replied.

David went to his pack. He was surprised at how hungry he was. His pack held all of his snacks, lunches, and his share of the group food. He rummaged through his pile of neatly labeled zipper lock bags.

"Is my mother compulsive, or what?" Willie commented.

"You helped her," David pointed out.

"Not with all these labels," Willie said. "It reminds me of when she pinned my name on my shirt for the first day of kindergarten." Willie carried his snack to the edge of the cliff. David looked at his own snack. The labeling was a little extravagant: "DAY 1 - MORNING SNACK - DAVID."

"I must have eaten too fast," Mr. Thurman said to no one in particular.

David saw Mr. Thurman massage the center of his chest with his finger tips.

"Look at this," Willie shouted. He stood at the edge of a thirty foot sandstone cliff, pointing to his left.

David urged himself to a stand again and walked to the nearest edge, about forty feet from Willie. Below him he saw a steep ramp leading into what appeared to be an abandoned mule corral.

He looked up and noticed Jay approaching Willie from the rear. Willie's hands were now in the pockets of his oversized, purple nylon shell jacket. Jay grasped the loose nylon fabric of Willie's jacket, careful not to alert Willie of his presence. David's inkling of what might follow tightened his stomach in vague nausea. With a casual, "Oops!" Jay shoved Willie toward the yawning abyss. Willie gasped, but could not free his hands from the jacket pockets. As his center of balance passed beyond the edge of the tan cliff, Willie squeezed his eyes shut. Jay hauled him back to safety with his powerful right arm.

Willie regained his footing and spun around, staring up hatefully at Jay. "You asshole," he spat.

"Watch your mouth, Willie," his father said, still fussing with his feet.

Willie returned to his pack at the rest house. When he finally looked up at David, there was a tear in Willie's eye. David shrugged his shoulders.

"God dammit!" Jay muttered. "A squirrel ate through the zipper." His unattended fanny pack would no longer close. Jay threw the useless zipper slide over the cliff.

"Watch the French," Mr. Thurman advised him.

"Oh, sorry, Mr. T," Jay replied, without the slightest pretense of sincerity.

"Fucker," Willie mumbled.

Following the rest break, David intentionally lagged with Willie at the rear of the party, since Jay tended to walk near the front, with the girls. They wandered with little elevation change through the seemingly endless ledges and slopes of the Supai as it headed toward the top of the massive Redwall cliff, near Cope Butte. In some of the minor drainages, David found the trail obliterated by rock slides. They boulder hopped from where the trail vanished, guessing where it might reemerge. The notion of a rock slide was unsettling to David. His attention alternated between his footing on the boulders and the threatening rocks above.

After making his way across the third rock slide, David stopped and waited for Willie. Looking back, he watched as Willie struggled from one tipped block of sandstone to the next. The three foot blocks of the rock slide appeared from David's vantage to be the remnants of a stone building, toppled yesterday, clean and square. But the stunted pinyon and pale green desert thorn that reached between the stones spoke to David of decades rather than days.

"What are you looking at, Davie?"

"Fifty million years of rock."

"It's that old?"

"No. That's how long it took for the layers of mud and sand to turn into the rock that's above us."

"Jeeze, we're only a little ways down."

"Yeah. The campsite tonight is another three hundred million years away."

"That makes my feet feel better. Thanks, Davie."

"Down by the river, the rock is something like two billion years old."

"Big deal. I'll be sixteen years old in August."

"I'm impressed, Willie. Your age and mine together, add up to less than that runty pinyon."

David walked with growing fatigue. His thighs did not ache, but their strength seeped away with the constant undulation of the trail. Even though the trail seemed to descend very little over the last hour, it was never level. David climbed and descended each rise with less energy than the last. Through the relentless Supai, he realized that the worst was still ahead: the five hundred foot cliff of the Redwall.

"There's my dad," Willie puffed.

David looked up. "The others must have gone on." David waved in response to Mr. Thurman's raised hand. When they reached him, David saw that Mr. Thurman was breathing hard and dripping with sweat.

"How long you been waiting, Dad?" Willie asked.

"About fifteen minutes. What happened to you guys?"

"Aliens," Willie replied with indignation.    "Aliens kidnapped us, honest. But we escaped."

"Oh," Mr. Thurman said, his attention on cutting another circle of moleskin. "That's a relief. For a second I thought you were just slow."

"Holy crap!" Willie looked down to the cascade of vicious switchbacks below.

"The maps call that the Cathedral Stairs," David pointed out.

"I feel closer to God already," Mr. Thurman grumbled, replacing his boot.

Despite David's exhaustion, he thought Mr. Thurman looked even worse. David recognized doubt in Mr. Thurman's face as the man forced himself to his feet and down the Cathedral Stairs. Willie followed, appearing to have difficulty descending the switchbacks without the aid of a walking stick.


Staff Sergeant Jeffrey Horn moved with urgency along the trail that trended east on the plateau of gray-green shale. The hiking here felt comfortable to Horn. More comfortable, at least, than the harrowing stretch of ice above, or the thousand foot slide down the precipitous slope that brought him to this plateau. Now he was pressed by the need to backtrack east as far as possible without being seen.

After two hours on the plateau, Horn descended a deep side canyon. He found a deserted campground beside a creek. At its south end was a walled double latrine. Inside, Horn found no toilet paper. His scraps of salvaged paper were nearly gone. The marked trail climbed to the East. With his capless Clorox bottle in one hand, and stolen walking stick in the other, Jeffrey Horn turned instead into the creek bed and headed into the inner gorge.


At the base of the Redwall, with Cope Butte high above to his right, David gratefully descended the switchbacks of the Muav and walked out onto the gentler slope of the gray-green Tonto Platform. He and Willie headed west toward the campsite at Hermit Creek. With the steep, broken Hermit Trail behind him and his spirits rising, he and Willie walked a little faster and spoke lightheartedly of classmates, movies and video games.

David stopped at the junction of the Tonto Trail with the trail that descends the inner gorge to the Colorado River at Hermit Rapids. In the late afternoon light, the pie crust layers of the one hundred foot thick Tapeats cliff below him appeared to yawn black and ominous.

"Don't even think about it," quipped Willie, as he walked past David.

David passed a deserted ranger cabin and the ruins that he knew to be old Hermit Camp, then finally rounded the last switchback to Hermit Campground. It's not paradise, he thought. He saw only a scattering of flat earth patches, separated from one another by lines of small stones and prickly pears. At the south end, David was happy to see, stood a glorious, walled latrine: his and hers. In the campground he saw no one other than the rest of his hiking party.

His first order of business was to remove boots and replace them with his camp slippers. This done, he and Willie pitched their tent.

"Yo, Alicia," Willie said, "You and me are supposed to fix dinner tonight."

"Make me puke," Laura commented. "Don't turn your back on him, Alicia, or we'll all starve."

"Don't worry," Willie retorted, "you can always find your usual diet up there." He indicated the latrine.

"You're so cute," Laura added.

David surveyed the scattered packages of food strewn about the campsite. "They suggest that you hang up all your food so the critters can't get into it. They can smell it a mile away, right through the plastic bags." It was a timid comment that David hoped would not sound too much like his own mother.

Jay looked at the damaged zipper of his fanny pack, which lay carelessly on the ground near the tent he shared with Mr. Thurman. Without acknowledging David's suggestion, Jay walked over to the girl's tent and demanded, "Your empty stuff sacks, please." Jay collected various sized stuff sacks and proceeded to pack the food for the remainder of the trip and hang it from a metal bar.

"Chow time," Willie announced.

David brought out his margarine tub bowl and a Lexan spoon. He noticed that no one was dishing up the food. They stood silently looking from the food pot to one another. David looked in.

"What's it supposed to be?" he asked. "It looks like poached worms on a bed of their own droppings."

Alicia held up the yellow plastic wrapper marked, "Turkey Tetrazini." She pointed to it with one finger, smiled her broadest TV commercial smile and said, "Don't leave home without it."

Willie took a bowl full. The others followed.

"It's not too bad," David commented through a mouthful, "if you think of it as something else, like food."

"Just wait 'till you taste Christmas dinner," Mr. Thurman taunted.

"What is it?" Jay asked.

"Dad's kept it hidden," Laura answered. "It's like a majorly classified secret."

"Here's the dessert," Willie offered, bringing out what appeared to David to be chocolate Jell-O.

"I see you were serious about the latrine," Laura said with exaggerated enthusiasm.

Despite the complaints, David found himself hungrier than ever before in his life. He lapped up every smudge of food from his bowl. Looking around, he observed that absolutely nothing was left over.

When Mr. Thurman walked to the latrine, Jay asked in a low voice, "Want to go down to the rapids after he goes to sleep?" He tilted his head toward Mr. Thurman.

"I'm too tired to go anywhere tonight," answered Alicia.

"Ditto," said Laura.

"That's crazy, trying to climb down the inner gorge in the dark." David wiped the pots with a small yellow towel.

"I expected you and Willie to chicken out," Jay said.

"I'll go," said Willie.

David looked with disbelief at the silhouette of his companion. "So will I." David regretted his words as they left his mouth.

"But you can't tell your daddy about it, Willie," warned Jay.

"As if he cares," Willie replied.

With the pots done, David wandered off a short way with Willie, where they simultaneously baptized a boulder. "You're a dumb shit, Willie."

"It's just a short trail down to the river," Willie said, with encouragement in his voice.

"It's a pitch black cliff trail down a thousand foot gorge. You saw where it started back there."

"A trail's a trail, Davie."

"Like hell it is. I read about walking on a trail in the dark, but that was on dirt, where you can feel the trail with your feet. This stuff is all rock on the cliff trails."

"Yeah," Willie replied, "I saw that stupid little book you brought."

"And if you fall off and your head busts open like a melon, I'm going to climb down just so I can kick your body. I can't believe I'm going to do this. And my legs are like Jell-O already."

"Maybe he'll fall asleep and forget about it," Willie hoped aloud.

"When pigs fly," David retorted.

Twenty minutes later, David stuffed his aching, swollen feet back into his boots. He'd lace them when he was certain that Jay was really going through with this. He wore a six inch halogen flashlight in a fabric holster on his belt, but he was sure that the batteries would never last all five days if he used it the whole time down to the river and back tonight. He put his pint of water into his fanny pack, along with a compass, whistle, and bottle of water purification tablets.

David's shoulders sagged with resignation when he heard Jay's tent zipper quietly open. Jay emerged into the chill canyon air. No stars were visible through the overcast. "Willie give up?" Jay whispered.

"No, he's coming." David felt sick. He went over to his tent and tapped lightly on the fly rod. A little triangle opened at the top of the door. "I'm afraid he's gonna do it, Willie."

Without comment, Willie closed the flap, then slowly unzipped the door and came out.

David reluctantly laced his size-fifteen boots. When he stood, he was surprised to be standing nose to nose with Willie's sister.

"Hi, guys," Laura whispered.

"I thought you weren't going, Laura," said Jay softly, as the four of them proceeded out of the campsite.

"I thought you were just bullshitting," she answered.

David knew that Laura never allowed Willie to tackle a challenge that she was unable to match.

"Anyway, I couldn't sleep," she added.

Now there was the bullshit, David thought. He was so tired that he was almost asleep as he walked. "At least Alicia's not big on jumping off cliffs tonight."

He reached the trail junction leading into the inner gorge. Four flashlights came on as they stood looking first into the chasm, then at one another.

## TAPEATS

Willie Thurman was stuck. Before him loomed the thousand foot drop of the inner gorge. He looked up. Scarcely visible in the night sky, the South Rim of the Grand Canyon towered three quarters of a mile above him. Even back in Missouri, he felt small beside these three classmates. Here within the Canyon, he felt insignificant—helpless. He wasn't about to back down from Jay's dare. Not this time. Besides, with his sister present, he would never hear the end of it if he chickened out.

*Dad would really be pissed off if he knew about this. He would be even more pissed off if I was too much of a wimp to go.* "Just look at it as a business decision, Willie," he would say. "You don't just count the cost. You have to weigh the return on investment."

Willie was afraid of heights. At least at night he could just follow the backside of whoever was in front of him. Willie decided that he would rather hike into the inner gorge without being able to see the bottom as he walked. He was frightened. He felt the chill of sweat beading on his forehead in the near-freezing canyon air. There was a tightness in his stomach, just below his breast bone. He could hear his heart pounding.

"You lead, Willie," Jay said.

"Me?"

"What's the matter, Willie," chuckled Jay, "afraid you're gonna piss in your pants?"

That's possible, he thought.

Davie stood next to him on the brink of the inner gorge. "Let's just go back, Willie," he whispered, "this is really stupid."

Willie was certain Davie was afraid too, and had come out of friendship. But Willie also knew that he couldn't turn back, with or without Davie. *It's a business decision.* He stepped forward and descended into the blackness, guided only by a trembling three foot disk of light at his feet.

"All right!" Jay cheered.

He could sense that Davie was right behind him. He had the urge to reach back and hold on to him, but instead focused on moving forward into the blackness. He couldn't tell if Laura and Jay were following. But he didn't care.

"Willie...Willie, take my walking stick," offered Davie.

"Don't need it."

"You can use it like a blind man's cane."

"I don't need it, Davie," snapped Willie. *Just walk.* He descended three rock steps in the trail. The third had no bottom. He fell. He heard Davie gasp. Willie twisted his body and immediately collided with rock. He groaned.

Willie was confused and trembling. The pain in his right shoulder and hip made it difficult to sort out what had happened. Darkness disoriented him. The others were talking and shining lights. He rolled carefully onto his hands and knees and swallowed a sob. His pain receded to a distracting throb.

Picking up the flashlight by his knee, Willie stood and turned to face the gorge. He shined the flashlight straight down in front of his feet and saw nothing. He backed away from the edge. The light beam was swallowed by the abyss eight inches beyond his toes. He realized that he had landed on a three foot ledge, seven feet below the trail. The ledge continued to his right another fifteen feet, where it seemed to rejoin the descending trail. *You don't just count the cost.* He gathered his frayed courage and side-stepped along the ledge to the trail, his shoulder and hip drumming his heartbeat in a dull rhythm of pain. He concentrated on slowing his breathing.

"You scared the living shit out of me," Davie said, his voice wavering.

"I'll take that stick, Davie." Businesslike. *It's a business decision. Just another day at the abyss. Seen one near-death experience, you've seen 'em all.*

As Willie proceeded, he discovered to his relief that the stick struck bottom on the ledges before he could see them clearly. Willie's confidence grew. His speed increased from timid creeping to a slow walk. The darkness yawned at his left, and pain lingered at his right, reminding him with each step how unforgiving the Canyon could be. He knew that he had cheated the Canyon once tonight. *I hope it doesn't hold grudges.* He descended a series of two and three foot shelves, and navigated the abrupt changes of course to the lower margin of the black, pie crust cliff that Davie had identified as the Tapeats.

"How much farther is it to the river, Davie?" Willie asked. Businesslike. *I'm the leader here.*

"About nine hundred feet."

Willie was accustomed by now to Davie quoting change in elevation, to measure distance. So he assumed that he was still nine hundred feet above the river. *Holy shit!* Businesslike.

"How long is the trail?" he asked.

"I don't remember, but probably something like a mile."

Willie stopped at the rushing edge of Hermit Creek and raised his light toward the Tapeats cliff, with its sliver of dark sky above. Three other lights followed, as Willie silently examined the impossible cliff above him. He thought about the inevitable climb back up. *Don't think about it!* He returned to the business of descent. He scanned the creek bank, looking for a place to cross the flowing, ten foot barrier, since the trail had ended at the water's edge.

"Back there," Davie said.

"Where?"

Davie guided Willie's arm, directing the flashlight across the creek to a stack of three small rocks.

"There," Davie said again.

"So?" Willie still saw no way across the creek.

"That's a cairn," explained Davie. "It marks a trail where there aren't any trees for regular trail markers."

"Ah," Willie replied in a businesslike voice. He side-stepped upstream along the sparkling black rock that sloped steeply into the water. When he reached a point opposite the cairn, he could see stepping stones beneath the water's surface. He tested them with Davie's walking stick, then bounded across.

Davie followed, but missed the second stone and plunged his right boot into twelve inches of flowing ice water. "Oh, shit," he blurted as he withdrew it and jumped to the far bank.

Willie continued down, the others walking in near silence behind him. *I'm the leader.* The trail crossed Hermit Creek at least a half-dozen more times, allowing one, then another of his followers to soak their feet, while he succeeded in keeping his own feet comfortably dry. As the slope of the descent became more gradual, Willie found that he was becoming proficient at locating the cairns with the narrow beam of light.

A quarter moon cast scant light into the haze above the narrow gorge, but it was enough for Willie to see the water and the margin of the sandy canyon floor on either side of the creek bed. The flashlights went out, one at a time, until he and his followers were all walking in darkness. Conversation had trailed off some time before.

Willie noticed the ribbon of dark sky widen above the towering, black rock walls. He sensed a rumbling. At first it was more of a feeling in his bones than in his ears. *Hermit Rapids!* A swell of victory washed over Willie, the sweetest he had ever savored. *I did it.* He had been the one to lead. He had challenged the dark, deadly cliffs and the fear within himself and had won.

He approached the violent roar of Hermit Rapids in the darkness. The vibration of its unseen power pulsed into his body from the ground. Willie was euphoric. *Someday, I'll tell Dad.* And he could prove it. Willie fumbled into his fanny pack and brought out a 110 camera. He pointed it toward the bank of the unseen Colorado River, still about twenty feet away, then angled it in the direction of the loudest roar from the rapids. He gently squeezed the button.

The discharge of the flash seared an image into Willie's mind: a beach, roiling brown water, its width receding into the darkness, and a man kneeling by the river. Now blinded by the flash, Willie could see only that frozen image. A kneeling man, a stranger, bearded and partly bald, not an old man, a stained denim jacket.

Without further thought, Willie apologized for the intrusion. "Sorry, I didn't know anybody was here. I was just taking a picture of the river."

Four flashlights trained on the man. his hand shielded his eyes. He seemed to have no gear with him, and if he had a flashlight, he did not use it.

In the awkward silence, Willie replaced his camera and shined his light on himself. *I'm the leader.* "I'm Willie Thurman...uh...we were just hiking down to see the...uh...rapids...We...uh...were not gonna stay very long."

"You're all just kids?" asked the squinting, bald man.

"Yeah," answered Jay in a baritone nearly an octave below Willie's cracking tenor.

Willie obligingly shined his flashlight over his companions.  As the four of them approached the man, all flashlights but Davie's were extinguished.  Davie shined his bright, fresh beam on the ground between them.

"You climbed down... in the dark... just to take a picture," the man stated, with a degree of admiration in his otherwise flat tone.

"You look like you been out here a long time," said Jay. "How long you been hiking?"

"A few days."

Willie sensed the man's reticence.

"How much longer you gonna stay?" Jay continued.

"You're full of questions," the man said with some irritation.  He paused.  "One of you kids wouldn't happen to have a spare canteen, would you?  Some of my gear got lost... in the river."

To Willie's surprise, Davie unzipped his fanny pack, removed his empty pint flask, and held it out to the stranger.
"It's not very big," Davie said, "but it's better than nothing." With his other hand, Davie brought out a tiny bottle of water purification tablets, letting his flashlight dangle from the shoelace tethered to his belt.  "I've got more in my pack," Davie added, nodding his head toward the creek gorge.

The man stared into Davie's eyes, then into Willie's eyes. In the swaying aura of reflected light, Willie saw what might be a tear brimming in the man's eye.  The man looked down at the flask and tablets in Davie's hands, then slowly took them.

The man lowered his balding head and said softly, "Thanks."  He turned, picked up a walking stick from the sand, and departed west along the beach.

Willie looked at the others.

"That's really weird... really weird," whispered Laura.

"I think we ought to get out of here," Davie said.  Davie sounded frightened.  "Like, right now."

No one argued.  Willie walked in silence up the drainage. With some degree of pride, he noted that the others automatically followed his lead.  In the dimming light from Willie's flashlight, he discovered that the cairns were much easier to see from below than they had been from above.  He moved quickly and silently for thirty minutes.  At the first rest, where the trail began its steep ascent, they broke their silence.

"Did you see the look in his eyes?" gasped Laura.

"What look?" asked Jay.

"I think he's that killer guy they were talking about on the radio," she added.

"That look in his eyes was gratitude," Davie mumbled.

"But the walking stick he picked up was Willie's."

"What?" Willie asked.

"I'm positive it was yours," Davie insisted. "You were the only one who took your stick out of the car last night. Remember?"

"Oh, God," Laura said. "You mean that guy was in our campsite last night? While we were asleep?"

"Son of a bitch!" Jay muttered.

"I think we ought to tell my dad," Willie suggested. To Willie, the situation seemed to warrant a breach of Jay's bullshit secrecy.

Jay put his index finger directly in front of Willie's nose. "You don't tell anybody; remember?"

"I don't know, Jay," Willie said, mostly to himself.

"Nobody!" Jay hissed.

With his sense of leadership diminished, Willie climbed in darkness, punctuated by illuminated searches for the elusive cairns marking the trail. An hour later, he reached the top of the Tapeats. Fatigue overwhelmed him. His mind was dulled from exhaustion. He mounted the sloping meander of the Tonto Trail and stumbled past the deserted ranger station and the ruins of old Hermit Camp, and finally to the entrance of Hermit Campground, near the walled latrine.

There, Willie stopped and stood in silence. He thought back over the three hours of brutal hiking. He had been physically drained by the day's hike before the descent into the inner gorge. Laura walked past silently and headed to the latrine.

Jay passed Willie and whispered loudly into his ear, "I hope that killer remembers which faggot took his picture." Jay continued into the campsite.

The euphoria, the victory, the sense of wholeness were gone. All Willie felt was fear and exhaustion.

When Jay was out of earshot, Davie said, "He's such an asshole, Willie."

Willie had no reply. Silently, they went into their shared tent, stripped, and climbed into their sleeping bags. Davie fell asleep in less than a minute. Willie thought about how foolish their secret excursion had been, and how close he had come to dying. *So close. Return on investment? Zip.*

For reasons that eluded him, Willie felt safer with Davie nearby. And that seemed strange, now that he thought about it. Davie was all length and no width. A light breeze would lift him from the ground. But still, Willie was glad that Davie was near.

In the twilight of the tent, he looked at Davie, who slept facing away from him, curled up in his sleeping bag. Did Davie also fault him for taking a picture of the man? Willie leaned over to see Davie's shadowed face, now slightly stubbled above the lip. Davie's hair was redolent with the sage-like smell of the Tonto, mingled with new sweat.

*Will that guy come to the camp again tonight?* The thought both excited and frightened him. Willie faded into the depths of dreamless sleep, comforted by Davie's proximity.

## MONUMENT

David Cadranel awakened. He had to pee. Pre-dawn light filtered through the green nylon of his tent. The only sound he heard was that of water tumbling over the rocks of Hermit Creek, thirty feet below his tent. He climbed out of his sleeping bag and unzipped the tent door slowly. No one else was up. He stepped out of the tent barefoot, wearing only his briefs. The temperature felt close to freezing. He quickly padded over to a nearby willow and relieved himself. On his way back, David saw his pint flask, the one he had given to the strange man at the river, now protruding from his fanny pack, which lay on the ground. Fear gripped him. He looked around the campsite and the surrounding hills, then walked to the edge of the ravine above Hermit Creek and looked up and down the creek.

David remembered that he and Mr. Thurman were supposed to cook breakfast today. The idea of doing it alone, before Mr. Thurman had an opportunity to harass him, seemed like a good plan. He looked around the campsite once more, then returned to his tent and dressed.

He untied the stuff sacks from the metal bar, and emptied them of all the zipper lock bags and prepackaged backpacker meals. He held up a yellow plastic package marked with a piece of masking tape labeled, "DAY 2," and read its front panel.

"Scrambled Eggs with Bacon Bits." He searched for the other package of the same food, since each contained only four servings.

"It's not here," he said aloud.

A trail of red powder trickled from a plastic bag of cherry drink mix. On examining the bag, David found one tiny hole made with tiny teeth. The stuff sacks had been suspended by their drawstrings, so none had an opening larger than a dime. Some tiny varmint that could fit through the opening must have a sweet tooth, he thought.  Then his thoughts returned to the man at the river.

Willie emerged from the tent, visited the willow tree, then staggered over to David.

"I feel like shit," Willie said.

"You look like shit," David replied.

"Thanks."

"Willie, that man was here during the night."

"How do you know?"

"One of the two breakfast packs is missing."

"You think he stole it?"

"And my pint flask is sitting by the tent."

"Holy shit," Willie whispered.  He looked around the campsite. "Is anything else missing?"

"One of the two packages of supper for day three, and, I think, some of the snack bags, unless Jay swiped them yesterday."

Wearing sneakers with his feet on top of the heels, Mr. Thurman flip-flopped his way over.  His thinning hair stood out straight in several directions. "What's the trouble?"

After David explained what was missing, Mr. Thurman roused the rest of the party, instructing everyone to bring out all the gear that each carried, and arrange it on the ground.  When everything was counted, the list of missing items had expanded to include a stuff sack, the second stove, a bottle of fuel, a cigarette lighter, a small cooking pot and three one-quart water bottles.

"Some son of a bitch must have snuk into the camp while we were asleep," Mr. Thurman pointed out.  "Did anybody notice anything?"

David and Willie exchanged glances.  David noticed Jay glaring at both of them.  David walked to his tent and calmly lifted his pint flask so Jay and Laura could see it.

Alicia joined the group. "What's happening?"

"I'll tell you later," Laura said.

"Well, I'll be damned."  Ranger Bill Gluzack perused the remaining printouts, then walked over to the front desk of the Backcountry Reservations Office. "Maria," he said, "we need to clear The Corridor and close the trails."

Maria Sanchez listened expectantly.

"They changed their minds about that storm. It's going to hit us."

"Wait just a minute, Mr. Luria," she called to a backpacker about to exit the BRO, "weather bulletin." Then turning to Gluzack, "How big?"

"The forecast is for rain, falling temperatures and very heavy snow accumulation by morning," he read.

"Mr. Luria," Sanchez said apologetically, "We're expecting a blizzard to hit late tonight. It will probably close all the trails."

Reluctantly, the young man returned the polypropylene permit tag to Ranger Sanchez. "I better get back to Tempe before it hits."

"From the sounds of it," Sanchez added, "you might need twelve-point crampons and snowshoes to climb out tomorrow morning."

"Oh, well," Luria muttered, as he headed for the door, "Merry Christmas."

"Merry Christmas, Mr. Luria. Sorry." She had forgotten that today was Christmas Eve. Sanchez looked over the itinerary sheet spread over the counter. "I've got nobody at Cottonwood, and fourteen at Phantom and Bright Angel. Indian Garden's got..." She shuffled the papers. "one party of six and a solo." Everywhere else is empty, except for a party of six on the Hermit loop, and they're not due to climb out for four days."

"Bring out everybody, except the Hermit party." Gluzack had apparently reached another quick decision. "Call them all now and have them get everybody going, ASAP. And let Cottonwood know what's going on.

"Oh, and we have another small headache. Sergeant Horn has been tracked to Boucher Trail. He's probably hiding in the no-man's land between Boucher and South Bass."

"What if he heads east?" asked Sanchez.

"That's not real likely, if he took Boucher. But I'm sending pairs of armed rangers down Bass, Boucher and Hermit, to pin him down. And there's not the slightest chance he could cross the river right now, even if he wanted to go north."

"Just six rangers for all that canyon?"

"Until the storm passes, that's the best we're going to do. Besides, I don't want to have to med-evac a bunch of federal marshals with broken legs."


Staff Sergeant Jeffrey Horn unbuttoned his stained, fleece lined denim jacket. He sat on the edge of a room-size erosion cave near the lower margin of the Tapeats. He had been walking for about four hours since leaving the river. From this vantage point, he could see anyone moving into this side canyon along the steep switchbacks down the eastern face of the Tapeats, and by looking to his left, toward the river, he could watch the trail entering from the plateau to the West.

Beside him lay a stuff sack that was now his pack. A small empty pot remained on the cold, wire-legged stove, its fuel bottle still attached. He was feeling better, thinking more clearly since eating his first real meal in three days. SSgt. Horn had prepared half of a food pack intended to feed four. He would save the remainder and try to stretch it out to last three or four days. He would have to fill in the gaps with whatever he could find.

He recalled the lecture he had given once a week for eleven months:

*"To survive, you will have to overcome being squeamish about what you eat. During your survival experience, you will be given the opportunity to sample some unfamiliar foods. Anybody ever eat rabbit?"* *Many hands are raised in the lecture hall.* *"What's it taste like, Lieutenant?" he asks, pointing to one student.*

*"It tastes like chicken," the student answers confidently.*

*"That's right, it tastes like...chicken. Anybody ever eat frog legs?" Fewer hands go up. "What's it taste like, Captain?"*

*"It tastes like chicken," she answers.*

*"That's right, Ma'am," he repeats, "It tastes like...chicken! Now, what do you think a roasted grasshopper tastes like, class?" he shouts, raising his hands to his ears.*

*With a booming chorus of fifty voices, the students shout in return, "It tastes like chicken!"*

Those lectures seemed a lifetime ago, as SSgt. Horn looked south to the massive Redwall cliff towering above the head of the side-canyon. Everything above and beyond it—the rest of the world—had ceased to exist, hidden by clouds and time and the events that had ended the life he had known.

He remembered the harrowing experience the day before, of hiking the trail along the western slope of Hermit creek. What he had not counted on was having to walk along an ice covered trail at the very edge of the upper formations. He was certain that, had he been wearing a backpack, he would have fallen to his death.

He recalled Hermit Creek, where his Clorox bottle slipped from his hand and washed into the rapids. He had found himself, then, at the bottom of the inner gorge with no food and no water bottle.

He had considered, last night, the pointlessness of trying to continue his flight, but drowning in the dark rapids had not seemed to be an alternative. He had thought of hiking up in the morning to find a sufficiently high cliff and ending it all that way. He had been too tired that night to climb back up the gorge, and was afraid that, if he had, he might have fallen in the dark and doomed himself to days of agony before he died.

That was the moment the four kids had surprised him by the river. Horn still found it hard to believe that they had climbed down the inner gorge in the dark just to take a picture of the rapids. The smallest boy, with the loosely curled hair, blue eyes and braces, had seemed so vulnerable. The little fart had actually apologized for the interruption. And the tall, skinny kid had given him, without hesitation, a new chance to live, another opportunity to think things through. They had saved his life without needing to know who he was.

He had felt strange this morning when he stole some of their food and equipment in the early dawn. He knew there was no other way for him to make it out of the Canyon. They would get by with less.

Horn scooped up a handful of sandstone dust from the shelf of the cliff and dumped it into the cooking pot. He stirred it around to scour the remaining food particles, then scattered the dust from the pot with a sweep of his arm. Using the free end of the stuff sack, he wiped away the traces of dust.

In the solitude, he stood. With a powerful tension in his arms and legs, Jeffrey Horn practiced the Sanchin exercise. Of all his martial arts studies, this keystone of Goju-ryu was his favorite way to release pent up stress.

He walked to the northern edge of the shelf, to gaze toward the hidden river below. A quarter mile down, near where he had entered this side canyon from the West, stood a solitary pillar of sandstone, over one hundred feet tall. It reached skyward from a base of pink and black granite. Judging from the contour of the gorge, it seemed likely that a man could find a way to the river from here. If he were able to find a way across the raging water, he could head toward the sparsely populated, high plateau of northern Arizona and Utah. But the river presented him with a barrier as formidable as the thousand foot cliffs. It seemed to Horn that the access to the river afforded by these side canyon descents always led to a portion of the river with vicious rapids surrounded by impassable granite cliffs.

He had considered attempting to swim across one of the smoother sections. But after putting his hand into the water for a few seconds yesterday, he was convinced that the muscles of his arms would be rendered useless from the cold long before he reached the far side. It would be impossible without some sort of raft.

The only way for him to cross would be over the bridge. He knew that there was a bridge across the river, somewhere in the Park, but he was unsure not only of its location, but also of his own location. The posted names of the creeks and side canyons meant nothing without a map.

Jeffrey Horn decided that he would cross the bridge at night, if he could locate it. Otherwise he would climb out the South Rim during the severe weather that seemed to be brewing above the rim.

He returned to his stolen gear and gathered the partially used envelopes of food, then looked for its yellow plastic outer bag. It was not there. He placed everything into his stuff sack and climbed down to the campsite below.

After ten fruitless minutes of searching for the lost yellow wrapper, Horn gave up. He realized that he had made an error in his evasion technique. By not placing a rock on the wrapper to keep it from blowing away, he had offered his pursuers an opportunity to find the wrapper and know that he had passed this way. He would not repeat that mistake again.


When David passed the junction with the Hermit Trail, in their backtrack eastward along the Tonto, he enjoyed a sense of relief. Hiking the steeply undulating meanders of the Tonto was considerably easier than climbing the Hermit Trail, either up or down. He continued east on the Tonto and climbed the pass below Cope Butte.

Cameras came out to capture the rare view of over a mile of the Colorado, looking upstream. Willie took a close up of David. Mr. Thurman snapped the whole group against a background of nondescript shale slope using the auto-timer on his 35mm camera, which he had balanced on a small boulder.

After the others continued, David framed the diminutive figure of Willie alone in one corner of the viewfinder of his pocket camera, with the river one thousand feet below and the unending canyon filling the rest. It left him with a foreboding that depressed his mood. Willie seemed so small and powerless, surrounded by the insatiable forces of the Canyon.

He began a gradual descent north toward the head of the next side canyon, passing along the eastern slope of Cope Butte. David was fascinated by the human-like stone pillars standing along the ridge connecting the butte to the main body of Redwall.

"Look at that, Willie."

"It looks like an audience watching us perform," said Willie.

"They must have gotten too many blisters and decided to just wait for a taxi," David quipped.

"Davie, look at that one." Willie pointed to their left.

"That must be why they call this 'Monument Creek'," David conjectured. Before them, stood a solitary, one hundred thirty foot pillar of sandstone upon a base of pink and black granite.

Across the gorge of the side canyon, vertical streaks of black Vishnu schist alternated with pink, vertical intrusions of Zoroaster granite, forming the unscalable wall of the inner gorge. Behind the pillar, three unusually wide bands of pink were joined at the bottom, forming a grotesque, three fingered hand that appeared to support the hundred foot layer of horizontal Tapeats on its fingertips.

The Tapeats cliff rested in lazy, crumbling layers, dozens of layers, perhaps hundreds of layers. All the layered canyon cliffs above were newer, younger, much younger, David knew. But the black and pink Vishnu seemed to stand frozen in streaks and folds of tortured compression. The Vishnu, with its tiny sparkles of mica and shiny, pink streaks and swirls of granite, appeared to be so much more permanent than the dull layers above it. To David, it seemed odd that both could be cleaved, with equal ease, into the dark gorge that spanned the length of the Canyon, reaching into each of the countless side canyons.

The Monument was an improbable collection of misshapen, brown stones precariously stacked to a height of one hundred thirty feet. Its base seemed narrower than its top. A gust of wind, David thought, could easily bring it all crashing to the floor of the side canyon. Yet it had stood there, at least long enough to be shown on the maps of the Canyon, long enough to have given this side canyon its name. At its top, David could see a small stack of stones, a cairn.

The others had passed out of sight, descending through the Tapeats on the western side of the Monument Creek drainage. David and Willie walked together, Willie in front. The dark brown crusted layers of the Tapeats soared above.

Looking over to the Monument again, David realized that it was nothing more than an island of Tapeats. He shuddered at the scale of time, measured in millions of years, required to sculpt this single column of sandstone from the surrounding cliff. David felt insignificant.

## COLORADO

David and Willie found the others standing nervously, engaged in a quiet discussion. They all turned toward the straggling hikers. Alicia held a yellow plastic bag that was labeled "Scrambled Eggs with Bacon Bits."

"Where did you find that?" Willie asked.

With a brief hesitation, Alicia answered. "There's no latrine, so I went up there to use the alternate bathroom, and this was just sitting there in the weeds."

"Your sister...and Alicia," Mr. Thurman explained to Willie, "are not comfortable staying at this campsite tonight, so we've all agreed—all of us that were here—to hike on down to Crystal Rapids and camp there."

"Camp at the rapids?" asked David.

"The map shows a campsite down there," Jay interjected.

After several minutes of discussion, Alicia suggested they discuss while they walked. So David followed the others back to the Monument and climbed down the precipitous switchbacks along its north western shoulder, leading them to the floor of the side canyon. They walked easily along the compacted sand in some areas, and with difficulty over fields of boulders in others.

"I heard they can give you like a parking ticket if you camp at the wrong place," Jay rambled.

"And you believe that?" Alicia asked, rolling her eyes.

"It's what I heard from Oscar Tomlin," Jay continued.

"They camped at a different campsite than the one on that tag, like Mr. T's got on his pack, and the rangers gave 'em a fifty dollar ticket."

"I'm afraid I don't believe that," she repeated.

"You don't have to. Just ask Oscar when you get back."

"Whatever," Alicia sighed. She moved closer to Laura and farther from Jay in the line of march.

The weight of the Canyon bore down upon David as he moved deeper into the inner gorge. He recalled his fear of the previous night's hike. Because of the darkness, it had been devoid of the magnitude and incomprehensible distances. He turned and looked back up the gorge of Monument Creek. Eight hundred feet above him and a mile away rested the base of the Redwall, with its five hundred feet of sheer cliff towering above. This alone dwarfed the tallest buildings David had ever seen. Yet beyond the inner gorge and Redwall, and three times higher, the buff colored cliffs of the Coconino floated in the mist, their tops capped with white. David again felt small and unimportant. He accelerated his pace to catch up with his companions.

Crossing a final boulder field, they stood at the edge of the Colorado River. The rumble and hiss of Granite Rapids filled David's senses with the frightening power that had carved and scoured away a thousand feet of solid granite, creating its own prison walls. The river frothed and boiled its mud-laden waters over the piled boulders beneath its surface.

A patch of sandy beach extended one hundred yards to the West, bounded by precipitous black slopes of Vishnu schist mingled with pink swirls of Zoroaster granite. To the East lay a field of ten foot boulders. David saw no campsite on the beach.

"I think it's over here Dad," called Laura from one of the huge boulders, where she stood alongside Alicia. "There's a path into those trees."

With his full backpack, David hopped over fifty yards of massive, smooth stones to arrive at what appeared to be a tunnel through a thicket of seep willows. Thirty feet into the thicket, the path widened into a stairstep nesting of tent sites sandwiched between the water on the North and steep, pink and black walls to the South. A pair of soft, flat sites near the water was immediately occupied by Mr. Thurman and Jay, and by Laura and Alicia. David preferred to camp away from the others, so he and Willie chose a site two steps higher, against the rising cliff. The dense seep willow cover was interrupted in several places by a view of the upper canyon and graying sky.

After pitching his tent, Mr. Thurman extracted a plastic jar from a side pocket of his pack and called everyone over to a solitary willow near the center of the area.

"It's Christmas Eve, so it's time to decorate the tree." He produced a string of miniature Christmas lights, powered by two

D-cell batteries. "Somebody do the lights." He handed it to Laura. "And these are your Christmas presents."

From the jar, he lifted a half-inch high, wooden, apple-shaped ornament suspended by a tiny loop of string. He handed it to Jay, and distributed four more to the others. The final ornament, his own, was a puffy, white fabric snowman ornament about three inches tall. When the lights and ornaments were in place, Phil Thurman ceremoniously switched on the lights, to the applause of the others. "Christmas dinner will be served in thirty minutes."

"Isn't Christmas dinner supposed to be tomorrow, Mr. T," Jay asked.

"When you see it, you'll understand," answered Mr. Thurman.

"What is it?" Jay was clearly interested.

"A surprise."

David wandered with Willie toward the boulder field that separated the campsite from the mouth of Monument Creek.

"Think you could swim across that, Davie?" Willie gestured toward the raging water.

David studied the rumbling brown mass that heaved and sloshed its way through the shadowed gorge. Waves rose in widely scattered hillocks of water that neither broke nor progressed downstream. Two small valleys in the dark surface remained unfilled by the surrounding flow. The far side appeared deceptively close. Looking upstream and downstream in the waning light, he estimated the distance to be at least a hundred yards of clawing and sucking river that could not be warmer than forty degrees. Awaiting the successful swimmer at the opposite shore was a vertical palisade of black Vishnu schist rising precipitously a thousand feet toward the abrupt, hundred foot Tapeats cliff, which capped the inner gorge. He turned and looked behind. The only differences between the north and south shores of the river were the gorge of Monument Creek, which offered an exit, and the gravel and rock that had once been a part of the side canyon, but had spilled, over eons, into the river to form the beach to the West and the boulder field on which he stood. The near edge, the water swirled gently around branches of small shrubs that must have recently grown from drier ground now submerged.

"Well," David finally said, "if you didn't get all your bones broken and your head crushed when the current sucked you into the rapids, you'd probably get too cold to swim before you got halfway across. And if you did get across, I don't see too many places over there where you could even climb out. I don't see any beaches on that side. It doesn't look like there's anywhere with even a little ledge to crawl up on."

"Does that mean no?"

"And if you did get across and did get out, you'd be two or three miles downstream by then."

"Wanna try it?" Willie asked with mock sincerity.

"Maybe in the morning. I hate drowning at night."

Willie touched David's arm to alert him to the scene on a boulder twenty yards away. Laura stood, leaning her back against a boulder, while Jay stood facing her, supported by one arm placed on the rock above her shoulder. They talked, holding hands.

David and Willie walked away.

"I thought they broke up two years ago?" David said.

"They did," answered Willie, "kind of suddenly. I think they went a little too far on a Sunday afternoon when nobody was home. Laura got scared, and broke up with him."

"What do you mean by a little too far?"

"You swear not to tell anybody?"

"Willie...."

"Well, one time, when I was over at your house doing Dungeons and Dragons, and my parents were gone, I think they went downstairs to the rec room and he screwed her."

"They were thirteen then," David protested.

"When I got home, she was acting all weird and bitchy and guilty looking. In the rec room I found one of her used tampons on the floor by the sofa."

"Jesus. What did you do."

"I flushed it down the toilet, so Mom and Dad wouldn't find it. Dad would have ripped Laura into little pieces, and then chopped Jay's balls off. Of course, that was before I decided that his balls ought to be chopped off."

"Did she know you found out?"

"No."

"I didn't think I saw overflowing gratitude in the way she treats you."

"She is kind of a bitch, isn't she?" Willie agreed.

"Have you ever done it, Willie?"

"What?"

"You know, made it with a girl."

"Sure. Lots of times. How about you, Davie?"

"Sure."

"How many times?"

"Lots," David answered. "Probably as many as you."

"Six?"

"You're such a friggin liar, Willie. You're a virgin and you know it."

"And like, you're not."

David couldn't see any point in continuing the discussion.

"Who do you have the hots for, Davie?"

"Okay!" exclaimed David, "now we're in my area of expertise."

"What?"

"Fantasy." David thought a moment. "I asked Hannah Snyder to the Christmas dance."

"She's pretty cool. What'd she say?"

"She said, 'Eat shit and die!'" They both laughed. "How about you?"

"I asked Wanda to that dance, and she said she would go," Willie confessed without hesitation. "But did you see her there?"

"I didn't go."

"Well, she canceled at the last second. Her little brother told me that she sat at home and watched a movie. I wonder if it's worth the humiliation."

"Willie...Davie," Alicia called, "tell everybody it's time to eat."

"Laura, chow time," Willie yelled, as if he were unaware of her location.

On returning to the campsite, David was astounded by the food spread out over a four foot, plastic Santa Claus table cloth, on the ground near the Christmas willow.

"This looks incredible," David exclaimed.

From the left, he lifted a slice from a pile of ham rising out of a three pound ham can. He topped it with a ring from a can of pineapple slices.

"Is that butter on the peas?" Alicia asked.

"Real butter," Mr. Thurman said proudly.

David served himself candied yams in heavy syrup from a tall scorched can.  Mr. Thurman poured punch into clear plastic cups printed with holly and poinsettias.  Into each cup he squeezed and dropped a slice of lime then plopped a maraschino cherry. *Green and red!*

For himself, Mr. Thurman opened a pint bottle of Johnny Walker Black Label, and poured a generous cup.

"Where'd all this stuff come from?" asked Jay.

"My pack," replied Mr. Thurman with pride.  "Lucky I had it inside my tent last night, instead of hanging with the other stuff."

"That all looks pretty heavy," David observed.

"Now you know why we're having Christmas dinner today instead of tomorrow.  Eat up, 'cause I'm not carrying any leftovers."

"No problem," said Jay, with unbridled enthusiasm.

"Hey, Cadranel, I thought Jew boys weren't supposed to eat ham."

"So?"

"So, how's it taste?"

"Roughly like bacon," David replied, "only less so."

"Oh."

David leaned to Willie's ear and whispered, "He's such a moron. I think he just now figured out that bacon and ham come from the same animal."

Willie snickered through a mouth full of candied yams.
David's family was not very strict about dietary rules, except for his uncle Nace.  It still made him uncomfortable to have the subject brought up by someone who, like Jay, didn't know what he was talking about.

When everyone was done, Laura cut the remaining ham into six pieces, and handed it out for dessert.  David dipped his piece into the leftover pineapple juice, then dredged it through the syrup in the yam can.  Since he felt uncomfortably full, and this piece of ham wasn't tempting enough to stuff into his mouth, he strolled away, holding it in his finger tips.

On a boulder near the water, David seated himself near Willie, and the two of them silently watched the darkening river surge past.  David leaned his head slowly toward Willie and whispered, "Look near my left knee."

A tiny mouse, no longer than two inches from nose to tail tip, walked directly up the vertical face of the boulder toward the piece of ham in David's left hand. David placed the ham on the rock without moving his arm. The mouse retreated out of sight, then reappeared moments later in the same spot. Its hurried movement alternated with four second rests of frozen immobility. Following three abortive attempts, the mouse reached the piece of yam flavored ham, took a corner of it in its mouth, then dropped it and retreated again.

"He realized it isn't kosher," David whispered. The mouse returned, nibbled a corner, retreated and continued this cycle for five minutes.

"He figured that it doesn't matter that it isn't kosher," David whispered, "since his mother isn't watching."

When the coated exterior of the ham was gone, the mouse ran off. David examined the tiny tooth marks on the ham. He realized that the critter that had found its way into the stuff sack and then to the bag of cherry drink mix, must have been a cousin of this mouse.

The rest of the freshman delegation approached David and Willie.

"So, Willie takes a picture with the flash. Boof! And this guy is, like, right there." Jay used his arm to exaggerate the proximity of the man at the river the night before.

"Now, why would an escaped killer let you take his picture, then just walk away?" Alicia pointed out.

Earlier in the day, David had overheard Laura telling Alicia about the whole thing, so he assumed that Alicia was doubting Jay's rendition just for the fun of it.

"Hi guys," Laura said to David and her brother.

"Is Jay telling you that bullshit about hiking to the river last night?" Willie was playing along.

"Very funny, gay wad," retorted Jay.

The five of them hopped along the ten foot silhouettes of boulders alongside the heart of the rapids. The roar made conversation difficult. In daylight, the massive boulders had each displayed a color that revealed to David its cliff of origin high in the canyon wall. In the twilight, a rock was either light or dark. Most were dark and polished.

Just behind Jay, Alicia screamed as she missed a step, slid between two boulders, and landed with her butt on a smooth flat rock.

Jay turned and applauded. "Way to go, Alicia."

Alicia dusted her jeans then extended a hand toward Jay, assuming he would assist her in getting back up onto the boulder. Jay looked briefly at the slender brown hand, then bounded away to the next boulder without comment.

"What an ignorant oaf," Alicia shouted.

Willie and David stepped over and held out their hands.

"Thank you," she said emphatically, returning to the top of the sloping boulder.

"I'll be right back," Laura shouted. She headed back to the campsite.

Jay moved near the water's edge, atop another boulder. "Christ!" Jay shouted, slipping from the boulder. "Son of a bitch! Somebody give me a hand."

Alicia was the first to reach the boulder from which Jay had slipped. She looked down and began to laugh. David and Willie reached a nearby boulder and saw Jay standing up to his knees in water. They joined the laughter. There were no footholds in the boulder face. Jay would have to walk in the water to make it around the next boulder.

"If you ass wipes are finished laughing, you can give me a hand," Jay shouted over the noise of the rapids.

With a broad, white smile, Alicia stooped toward him and clapped her hands.

David watched as Jay coiled and sprang in rage at Alicia. Jay's hand swiped at Alicia's left foot. With a gasp, she toppled forward and completely vanished into the water.

"Where the fuck did she go?" shouted Jay in amazement.

"Down stream," urged David, shoving Willie forward, "Go, Go!"

The two of them left Jay standing in the shallow water and rushed from one dark boulder to the next, pausing at the top of each, only long enough to look at the near edge of the rapids.

"She could be trapped under a rock," Willie shouted.

"Just keep moving," David answered, at the top of his voice. He felt panic sweeping over him.

"There, Davie," Willie pointed.

Five yards from the edge of the water, in the border of Granite Rapids near the mouth of Monument Creek, Alicia's shoulders rose against the force of the river.

"She's on the gravel bar," shouted David, still racing downstream along the boulders.

When Willie reached the trickle of water that was Monument Creek's present outflow, he jumped across to the gravel bar and headed toward the edge of the river.

"Don't go in," shouted David, joining Willie on the dry gravel bar. As he shouted, Alicia vanished again into the blackness. Neither of them carried a flashlight. He knew the sloshing rumble of the rapids would drown any call for help.

"Keep going," he yelled, pointing down stream.

David ran down the beach, west of the rapids, as fast as the sand would allow. He saw Alicia surface again in the water, coughing and thrashing her arms in an ineffective stroke. At the end of the beach, twenty feet down stream from Alicia, David could go no farther.

"Hold my hand," David shouted to Willie. He took two steps into the frigid river. "Swim, Alicia, swim."

He could not make out her face, but thought she was swimming more effectively. She was ten feet from the beach, and moving rapidly down stream. David took a quick glance at the dark margin of the river downstream. It was sheer cliff, he thought, until the break at Hermit Rapids, miles farther down. His heart pounded in his chest. The blackest fear gripped him.

"More," he shouted to Willie, as he stepped farther into the river.

Alicia's hand reached toward him. It glided past, six inches beyond his reach. As the river sucked at his feet, David plunged, full length, into the river, losing his grip of Willie's hand.

David held his breath as biting cold engulfed his body. He felt the denim of Alicia's jeans, which he grabbed desperately. He felt pain in his left ankle as his boot twisted.

David bent his left leg and drew his body toward whatever had caught his boot. The water continued to rush over his head. He held onto Alicia's jeans. Then he felt sand beneath his right boot.

*Willie!* It was Willie tugging at his left boot. David felt a hand grasp his belt and yank him backwards. As he fell onto

Willie, Alicia scrambled frantically, like a frightened kitten, up and over them. There she collapsed on the sand, crying, coughing and shivering.

It took David a moment to realize what had happened. Then he began to tremble. Willie was talking, but David couldn't understand what he was saying. Something about cold. Of course.

David helped the shivering girl to her feet and, with Willie's help, went to the nearby rock slope.

"We've got to get you warm," David said to Alicia, trying to penetrate the loud sobs.

They leaned her against the slope of granite, where David unbuttoned her soaking wool shirt. The shirt was halfway off when David became aware of the white sheen of Alicia's bra.

"Give me your shirt, Willie," he said through his clattering teeth.

"Uh, okay." Willie seemed shocked by the view of David undressing the beautiful girl.

David, who was meeting no protest from Alicia, removed her shirt and then stared, mystified by the bra. "How do you take this off?" he shouted to her.

Alicia reached up to the front center of the bra and unfastened it. David waited as Willie removed his jacket and then his sweatshirt, leaving him a T-shirt. David squeezed water from the wet sleeves of the sweatshirt, then pulled it over Alicia's head. He freed the bra straps from her shoulders, and with her mute help, got her into the sweatshirt.

"Give me your shell pants," he shouted to Willie. David swallowed hard, and went about unfastening her jeans. He pulled off her low sneakers, then struggled until the wet jeans came off. Alicia absently returned her glistening white underpants to their proper position. He then helped her into Willie's nylon shell pants.

"Why don't you wear my jacket, Davie," Willie offered.
David removed his wet shell and his shirt, and replaced them with Willie's purple jacket. They helped Alicia back into her sneakers, then gathered up all the wet clothes. With Alicia between the two of them, they headed east along the beach, toward the campsite.

"I'm...very...cold," Alicia stammered, "and my ankle...hurts."

David looked down and saw a small cut on the outside of her right ankle.

"Let's get her back to the camp," said David. "I think she has hypothermia. We need to get Laura to strip her down to dry underpants, and climb into the bag with her, skin to skin, until she warms up."

"What?" said Willie with amazement.

"It's the only way to warm her up," David answered.

"Dad!" Willie shouted. "Dad!"

"He's drunk." Laura's voice came from her tent.

"Laura..."

"Will you faggots get lost," Jay threatened, his voice also coming from within Laura's tent.

David saw the empty scotch bottle lying in the duff between the two tents.

"What do we do?" Willie whispered.

David looked at the blank expression on Alicia's face. Her lips appeared dark and slack. David pointed to the tent he shared with Willie.

"We can't do that," Willie said, his eyes wide.

"We have to, Willie. I'm freezing. Alicia's got to be colder. We have to."

Inside the tent, they unzipped both sleeping bags. David spread one bag on top of the other and guided Alicia between them. It worried David that she complied without protest, without even an awareness of where she was. He stripped off his wet clothes, replacing his briefs with a dry pair. Removing the nylon jacket Willie had loaned him, he crawled alongside Alicia.
"God, her skin is cold. Get undressed, Willie. We've got to warm her up."

"I don't know, Davie. This doesn't seem..."

"Dammit, Willie, just do it."

Willie undressed with obvious reluctance, and lay at Alicia's other side, beneath the cover. David pressed himself against her.

"Her sweatshirt is wet," David said. "Alicia. Alicia."
She didn't respond. David lifted her arms and pulled off the sweatshirt, then the shell pants, leaving her in only underpants. Willie said nothing, but David interpreted the silence as condemnation.

Once again, David pressed himself against her, his head resting on her shoulder. The horror caught up with him. He held Alicia's hand and cried silently.

"Davie," Willie whispered, "do you think she'll be mad at us tomorrow?"

"Maybe."

Listening to the Colorado River churn its way over Granite Rapids, David fell asleep.

## BLACK BRUSH

Willie Thurman lay with his eyes closed, listening to the gurgle and rush of the Colorado River, punctuated by the early morning calls of birds in the seep willows. He couldn't remember ever feeling so content.

The warmth of Alicia's hand on his abdomen felt wonderful. So tender, so gentle.

He clearly remembered going to sleep with his back toward her. Separating the dream from the reality of what followed was not as clear. Had she turned and kissed his lips with a fairy touch? Did he dream that?

Willie thought about the little bumps on her back, along the spine. They felt so alive, the softness of her skin and the firm movement of muscle beneath. She was so petite in her clothes, but seemed so large and real pressed naked against his body last night. Her fragrance, the smell of dust and sweat, had been that of the Canyon and the river.

Now her hand radiated warmth. With his eyes still closed, he gently caressed her hand and placed his other hand on her abdomen. They touched each other with tiny gestures. He was confused. Both hands snapped away simultaneously.

Willie opened his eyes and, inches from him, saw Davie looking back, a shocked expression on his face.

"Sorry," Davie whispered.

"Me too," Willie replied. Blood rushed to his head. He could see that Alicia was not in the tent. His contentment swirled into uncomfortable questions. He rolled over, trying to remember touching Alicia's breast last night. He felt pretty sure he had, but he wasn't certain. He wasn't certain of any of it now. It had been pitch black, and he had been exhausted. What had really happened? Maybe, he thought, Davie had made the same mistake he had, assuming that Alicia was still there.  *Or maybe Davie was shocked only because I was shocked.*

After putting on his long johns, Willie opened the tent door and circled around to the black stone cliff to pee.  Maybe it was all a dream.  How could he have felt so wonderful, but not even know what happened?  When he turned back around he saw the river.

During the night, the river had risen enough to reach the campsite.  Brown water was lapping at the rear of the other two tents.  His thoughts of love or humiliation or whatever they should be, evaporated in the heat of a more urgent matter.

Willie returned to his tent.  "Davie, wake up."

"Yeah?"

"The river is rising."

"What do you mean, Willie?"

"The river is up to the other tents."

Davie got up on his knees and looked out the open tent door.

"Wake up everybody, while I get some clothes on."

Willie jammed his bare feet into his boots and went from tent to tent, to awaken the others.

"God dammit," exclaimed Jay.

Willie found it curious that Jay's voice came from his dad's tent.

"The tent's all wet," Jay continued.

One by one, the others grumbled, then came out of their tents partially dressed.  Alicia was with Laura.

"Thanks, Willie, for last night," said Alicia, "It was all a blur."

*A blur?  God, if you only knew!*  Yes, he thought, she is beautiful and small and magical.  Her flawless face and firm little lips.  And those eyes that opened into a bottomless depth.  Her small, upright breasts, bra-less beneath a clinging tee-shirt, raised the question once more.  Willie could easily imagine savoring their warmth in his hands, but he couldn't remember the reality of having touched them.

"Davie pulled you out of the water," Willie stated, avoiding any discussion about their sleeping arrangements.

"My sleeping bag's wet," complained Jay.

"Ours are too," said Laura.

"Maybe you could air them out over on the rock slope," Willie suggested. He realized he was staring at Alicia, and feeling her thrill throughout his body. He turned away.

Willie's dad emerged from his tent and surveyed the campsite and the river. He walked through the willow tunnel path a short distance, then returned. "Forget about airing out the bags. Let's get packed up and out of here before we end up trapped."

"Is the path still clear?" asked Jay.

"Partly," Phil said, starting to pull things from their tent. "The river is rising, so we have to leave now."

Willie returned to his tent to get it down. He and Davie quickly packed the tent. To avoid Davie, Willie tended to the food hanging in the stuff sacks, sorting it into personal piles, then distributing it to the others.

As he passed the Christmas willow, he remembered that it was Christmas morning. Willie quickly decided that the tangled string of lights would have to remain. He plucked the six ornaments from the tree, then ran to Davie, who was frantically packing.

"Merry Christmas," he said to Davie, handing him the tiny, wooden apple. Willie looked at Davie's bony knuckles and impossibly long fingers. He couldn't make eye contact.

"Merry Christmas, Willie," Davie replied, almost apologetically. He placed it into a zippered pocket on his jacket.

"Merry Christmas," Willie said, as he handed an ornament to Jay, much as one might serve a third helping at a fish fry.

"Great," said Jay, as he flicked the ornament into the shallow edge of the river.

Willie went over to his sister's tent. "Merry Christmas." He handed each of the girls an ornament.

"Merry Christmas, Willie," said his sister, with a warmth Willie was unaccustomed to hearing.

Alicia stood and hugged him firmly. "Thanks," she whispered to him.

Willie didn't want to release her. The warmth of her chest against him caused a shudder to course through him. He couldn't think of a reply to match the intensity of the moment. He relinquished his one second embrace with a smile that felt awkward and juvenile.

Willie walked over to his father, who was folding the wet tent. "Here, Dad." He handed Phil the fabric snowman ornament. "Merry Christmas," he said, feeling as though he had to make some excuse to justify interrupting him.

"Willie," Phil barked, rubbing his head, "we're trying to get out of here."

"Right, Dad." Willie walked away. *And a Merry Christmas to you too, Willie my boy.* He placed the remaining ornament into his jacket pocket and zipped it shut.

With everyone packed, Willie watched, embarrassed, as his dad tossed the ham can and the other heavy items of trash from yesterday's dinner into the river. Then they headed through the tunnel path beneath the seep willows. Its western end was submerged. Phil Thurman headed to the granite slope, the others following. They shuffled along the steep slope, circumventing the boulder field, which was inundated by the turbulent brown water.

"I left my jacket at the campsite," Alicia said. She turned and ran back.


Alicia May Waters struggled to catch up with the others after retrieving her jacket from a willow branch at the campsite. She found that walking on the steep slope of black stone caused her right ankle to hurt. The rest of the party rounded the final pitch and passed out of sight up Monument gorge.

The cut on her right ankle was hurting more than she could tolerate. At a spot where a boulder lay near the slope, she stopped and removed her pack. She decided to loosen the boot and place a bandanna on the outside of her right ankle to relieve the pressure against the cut. She unzipped the pack's small lower compartment, which contained her clothes. After rummaging through it, she realized that the bandanna must be in the larger, upper compartment. She unzipped it and immediately located the bandanna among the packages of food.

Alicia sat on the boulder. The nearness of the rapids reminded her of the cold fear and hopelessness that had swallowed her last night—the terror, the panic. She remembered the unyielding power of the river. And the painful cold.

Alicia thought about her surprise at awakening, almost naked, sandwiched between Willie and Davie. She smiled to herself when she recalled that giddy feeling of recognizing that both of them were also sleeping in only their underpants. There they were, so proper, facing away from her.

She unlaced her right boot. Forming a doughnut with the bandanna, she placed it over the ankle bone, and began to lace the boot. It was at that moment the pack slid and tumbled, catching itself face down between the rock slope and the boulder. Alicia's heart stopped. She leaned over and grasped the nearest end of the pack frame. With a tug, she scraped the pack back onto the rock beside her. In the water below, Alicia's clothes slowly sank as they rotated downstream. Above them, the packets of food floated in their sealed, zipper lock bags. They were beyond her reach. She looked about, then seized her walking stick and attempted to stop the food from floating away.

First one, then another of the food packets dodged her stick. Alicia salvaged a single yellow packet labeled, "Beef Stroganoff," by trapping it against the black rock slope and guiding it slowly toward her. After sliding it upward on the slope, she was able to step across and catch it. She threw it into the empty upper compartment of the pack, then zipped it and the lower panel shut.

Alicia watched the elusive food packs drift into the rapids and out of sight, as she laced her boot. She thought of her riding stable in Columbia. How she wished she could mount her favorite chestnut mare, and ride out of this awful canyon. "Flower" would respond to her needs and desires, and would carry her up the canyon trails and gallop out into the snow above.

She lifted her nearly empty pack and settled it on her shoulders, mindful of leaving the hip belt unfastened until she was safely across the water. Davie had suggested that the day before, while crossing the trickle of Monument Creek. It had seemed ridiculous at the time. Now, with the horror of the smothering rapids fresh in her mind, she understood the truth of it.


"I see her now," shouted Willie, "she's coming." Willie and his dad had contoured high on the eastern flank of Monument Gorge to see if Alicia was catching up. The rest of the group had descended the crumbling rock slope, and were now walking up the valley's wandering trail.

"I think we have to go back the other way, Dad," said Willie, "The trail's gone up here." He looked back and watched Alicia slowly closing the distance between them.

"That's a lot of backtracking, Willie. We just need to get around this damn cactus, and the trail keeps on going."

The game trail on which Willie stood skirted a steep pitch of loose scree above and below. The stiletto spines of a three foot agave plant clearly blocked the path. By Willie's reading, a slip here would mean a sixty foot slide down the dirt and broken rocks.

Willie Thurman watched his dad move to pass above the agave, then back up and move around it from below, leaning his face away to avoid the spine tips. Willie saw the footing crumble beneath his dad. In a reflex move, the palm of Phil's left hand impaled itself on an agave spike, and inch of the spine protruding from the back of his hand between the thumb and index finger. Phil's feet seemed to dig into the dirt to halt his slide. Bracing himself with the walking stick in his right hand, Phil jerked his left hand off of the agave. The momentum of his arm threatened to carry him down the slope. Willie grasped his father's jacket, and pulled him against the slope, away from the dozens of waiting agave spikes.

"Oh, damn, that hurts," his dad finally groaned. Blood welled up from his palm and dripped from the exit wound on the back of his left hand.

Willie pulled a thin knit glove from his jacket pocket. "Here, Dad. Hold this in your hand to stop the bleeding." He placed the balled up glove against the entry wound and closed his father's fingers around it. Willie paused for a wave of nausea to pass. His dad's face appeared pale. "Are you okay, Dad?"

"Yeah, lets go back the other way."

Willie and his father contoured back along the narrow game trail to the point where the others had descended. There they met Alicia.

"What happened, Mr. Thurman?" Alicia asked, on seeing the blood dripping slowly from Phil's hand.

"Just got stuck on a cactus. Where have you been?"

"My ankle was hurting," she explained, "so I stopped to do something with my boot. Then my pack tipped over and some of the stuff fell into the river." She paused, biting her lip. "I got back some of it."

Willie read the distress in Alicia's otherwise perfect face.

"Well, girl," Phil said, "we'll figure it out later. I don't think I want to hear any more bad news right now." He headed down the slope, angry at himself or Alicia or Willie or everything. Willie could see only anger.

Willie walked with Alicia. "How's that cut on your ankle?"

"It really hurts. I kind of padded it, and that helps." She walked with a slight limp.

"What all got lost...out of your pack?"

She stopped walking. Holding back tears, she answered, "Everything. All my clothes and all the food and things. I got back one dinner pack."

"No problem, Alicia," he said in a cheery tone, "I've got an extra pair of socks and Davie has an extra shirt, and Laura can lend you..."

"What about the food?" she interrupted.

"You lost the other meal pack and, what, a couple of lunches."

"All three lunches and the snacks," she corrected.

"So, we'll share." He smiled and waited for her to return the smile. He accepted a dismayed smirk and added, "See? No problem, Alicia." Looking north across the river, Willie pointed out a magnificent temple illuminated by a ray of sunlight and framed between the dark walls of Monument Gorge. He felt wonderful beside her. They resumed walking.

"Your father seemed pretty angry."

"I think he was just embarrassed, because he jabbed his hand doing something stupid."

"How bad is his hand?"

"Well, that cactus spine, like that," he pointed to a nearby agave, "stuck all the way through his hand and came out the other side."

"Oh, no. That sounds really gross."

"He always gets, you know, kind of pissed off at everybody when he does something dumb. So I think he's madder at himself than he is at you. Plus he's probably got a hangover."

Willie had to know about last night. He turned a dozen questions over in his mind. "Last night..."

She looked at him with a strange and unreadable expression.

He continued. "In the tent...we had to take off all the wet stuff..."

"Willie, you saved my life."

"When did you leave?" He couldn't believe he asked that.

"When I heard Jay and Laura talking outside."

"Were you...okay?"

"I was fine, Willie. You turned a really scary accident into something nice." She smiled at him.

It was clear to Willie that she wasn't angry about last night, but he couldn't think of a way to ask her what happened between them. He would sound stupid no matter what the question. *God, she's beautiful!*

They climbed the switchbacks below the base of the Monument and found the others waiting. His dad had located the first aid kit. All the gauze pads were wet from the flood. Phil settled for a foil pack of povidone iodine ointment, which looked like old axle grease to Willie. Phil squeezed it into both sides of his wound, then wrapped his hand in soggy kling bandage. It bled slowly.

After a heated inventory of food and supplies, they headed up the gorge, watching for any signs of the person or people who had stolen their supplies the previous day. Willie had again fallen to the rear with Davie.

"Look at the snow," said Davie.

Above them, the others in the party climbed the steep switchbacks on the eastern Tapeats over Monument Creek. Beyond, and much higher, past the Redwall, Willie could see the upper reaches of the South Rim, its snow covered terraces extending much farther down the walls, into the Supai. The heavy clouds overhead appeared to roll furiously at the rim. The rim itself was lost to view. That seemed to Willie to be a fair representation of his relationship with Davie.

He climbed the Tapeats and shuffled along the Tonto without speaking. Davie was uncharacteristically silent. Willie could sense the tension between them. The gray-green shale slope of the Tonto reached from the steep talus of the Muav, which formed the foundation of the massive Redwall cliff, to the lip of the Tapeats. It seemed to Willie, that all the loose fragments ought to spill into the inner gorge, transforming the

Tonto into a flat deck, like the wooden stool in his sandbox, years ago, when he would pile the sand too high.

With each step, Willie's boots crunched the shale into slightly smaller pieces. This, he thought, is why the Tonto Trail appeared to be a duller color than the nearby stone: less green, more gray. The trail's texture seemed more like gravel than the rest of the slope, which resembled haphazard piles of broken flagstone.

He needed to know what had happened last night. Had he made-out with a beautiful girl? Or had she already left the tent. He couldn't think of a way to bring it up with Davie.

Evenly spaced over the slopes, shrubs of various unfriendly varieties grew in isolation, appearing to Willie as though a gardener had carefully measured the distance before planting each one at twenty foot intervals. He saw an occasional barrel cactus and some variation of prickly pear. Most of what grew here were homely, three foot wide nests of tangled, thorny branches bearing tiny clusters of dull, quarter-inch leaves. Davie had identified them earlier as blackbrush. They weren't really black, he thought. For all their lack of appeal, they might just as well have been black. Willie wondered if growing one in rich soil, with plenty of water, would cause it to be more attractive, or just kill it. He remembered a potted cactus in Columbia that was overwatered. It grew like a weed, until its own weight caused it to break in half.

Willie felt as though he were walking beyond the normal flow of life here. It could be yesterday, or a hundred years ago. The only thing that anchored Willie to the present was Davie, walking behind him. Even that was a tenuous connection now.

The scrub, the gray-green shards of Bright Angel shale, the barrel cactus, the occasional lizard, so far as Willie could guess, might have been the same for thousands of years. He recognized that he was an intruder here.

"Do you think I'm weird?" Willie asked.

"What?"

"Because of what happened?"

"When?"

"You know, last night, this morning," Willie said, finding it difficult to be very specific.

Davie appeared to find the subject uncomfortable. "I'm not sure I know what you mean, Willie."

"Neither am I," Willie said in truth.

"I mean, Alicia was there, almost naked, and then she was gone."

"Well, I fell asleep," Willie tried to explain, "and then I woke up and I thought Alicia was...I don't know."

"Do we have to talk about this?" Davie complained.

"I guess not." Willie was more confused.

They continued along in silence for twenty minutes.

"Willie."

"Yeah?"

"Did you know that I brought a stuffed rabbit?"

Willie turned his head around and smiled. "With you?"

"Yeah. I brought him in my pack."

"Are you serious?"

"I'm serious."

"Why?" Willie asked.

"Just before I left, I asked my mother if I forgot anything. She said, 'only your bunny,' as a joke. So, just to be funny, I went and got it."

"That's pretty strange, Davie."

"It's no stranger than packing in a whole Christmas dinner, complete with a canned ham."

"So, what's his name?"

"The rabbit? Ezra."

"Ezra?" Willie laughed so hard that he couldn't walk for ten seconds.

"He just looks like an Ezra."

They rejoined the party at Cedar Springs, where they stopped for a lunch of beef sticks, cheese sticks and mangled candy bars, shared evenly.

Willie pointed out the snow storm on the South Rim, but no one seemed interested. His father and Alicia were each focused on their painful injuries, touching and repositioning pads or bandages or socks. Laura and Jay were preoccupied with a polite public banter, rich with innuendo, as they tossed volleys of pea sized stones back and forth at one another.

Six of them sat together, but Willie felt as though he was the only one aware of them as a single group, struggling against the Canyon, against a strange bearded man with sad eyes. Most of all, he sensed them struggling against themselves.

They resumed their hike toward Salt Creek, where they planned to camp for the night. The endless, gray clouds seemed to steal from the Canyon its radiant hues of orange, yellow and buff. What remained was a devouring dreariness of grays and rust. The Redwall, always to Willie's right as he followed the narrow trace of the Tonto Trail, dominated the horizon, massive and impenetrable. Its sunlit glow of yesterday had degenerated into aging brick, pocked by unreachable caves five hundred feet above them. Smudged black patina wept from its face.

Willie unzipped his purple nylon jacket as the exertion warmed his hardening muscles. He felt the tiny wooden ornament in the jacket pocket and remembered today was Christmas.

Alicia Waters blushed as she sat upon the impossibly exposed throne latrine above the Salt Creek campsite. Laura stood her turn as sentry fifteen feet away. Even though Alicia could see at least a quarter mile in every direction, there might just as well have been eight foot walls. It's isolation, in the center of a Redwall bay called, "The Inferno," was threatened only by the possibility of someone hiking up from the small campsite eighty yards away. Even in the wilderness, Alicia was accustomed to the reassuring proximity of a bush or log. Here, the solitary, stainless latrine stool was situated atop a knoll, its dusty seat rising above the sparse blackbrush evenly dotting the crumbled shale.

She stood and pulled her clothes back together. "I've got to take a picture of this," she said to Laura, as they headed back down to the campsite, "Nobody will believe it."

"I don't believe it," added Laura, "and I just sat on it."

Alicia was favoring her right foot more, after the day's hike. As they approached the campsite, nestled among several huge stones tipped at odd angles, high on the west bank of Salt Creek, Alicia watched as Jay stalked, then threw a stone at a scrawny mule deer. He missed. The deer bounded off to the West.

"What's the matter, Jay," shouted Alicia, "did you run out of lizards to step on?"

He brandished the middle finger of his left hand.

"I think I'm just going to sit and put my foot up on a rock or something until supper."  Alicia limped to a particularly inviting boulder.

"You better wear an orange hat," Alicia suggested to Laura, "or Jay might throw a rock at you."

"Don't worry," Laura replied, "he always misses."

"Jay," Phil Thurman yelled.

"Yo, what's up Big T?" Jay asked.

"The creek is dry here.  I want you and Willie to get all the water bottles and walk down stream 'till you find the water."

"I'll take care of it myself, Mr. T."

"Willie, you go too."

"Dad," he complained.

"Go!" Phil ordered with a thrust of his index finger.

"Right," Willie responded.

"You get all the bottles, Willie," Jay said over his shoulder, "and I'll go look ahead."


Jay Vesco walked along the sand and gravel creek bed, following its gradual downward course.  He had to admit that it would have been odd if Mr. T had invited him to hike the Canyon without bringing along that little faggot son of his.  He guessed that Mr. T was hoping the trek would turn Willie into a man.  Fat chance of that.  *The whining little shit only has about seven pubic hairs and looks like he ought to be in the sixth grade.*  Jay wondered why he was always the one stuck with babysitting.

*And worse, Willie brings along that skinny, gay-wad freak, Davie.  He thinks he's hot shit just because he kisses the ass of every teacher in the school.*  Jay knew that his own grades would be straight A's if he would stoop to that.

And it was that curly haired little fuck, Willie, who had gotten him in trouble in seventh grade.  Jay remembered the stray cat he and his younger brother had dowsed with gasoline and set afire.  It seemed to Jay that it was no different than what the city pound would do.  Willie, he was pretty sure, had been the one who called the police.

Willie caught up with him.  "Doesn't look like there's much water down here," Willie said.

"Maybe down farther," Jay said.  He looked at the small boy.  *He's cute if you think of him as a girl.  Curly light brown*

*hair, blue eyes, smooth face, the glint of braces between his lips.*
He remembered two years ago catching Willie alone in the
garage. He had trouble deciding whether to bash his brains out
with the claw hammer or fuck him. But Mr. T had driven up the
driveway, so he let him go.

"So what do you and Davie do in your tent, Willie?"

"What do you mean?"

"Do you jack off, play with each other or take turns
humping?"

"Go to hell, Jay."

"Now you're gonna tell me the two of you aren't faggots."

Willie didn't answer. Jay didn't need an answer. *Why
else would Willie have invited such a worthless freak as Davie
to hike with him in a place like this?*

They walked on down the creek bed, past two rusty,
stagnant pools, and down several wet ledges.

After fifteen more minutes of walking and skipping down
zigzag stairsteps in the creek bed, they found water trickling into
a clear, fresh pool about eight inches deep. By that time, Jay was
pretty fed up with Willie's attitude. He left him at the pool with
the water bottles, while he explored farther down.

Jay walked out to where the walls of Salt Creek Gorge
seemed to widen abruptly. As he approached the edge, his
breathing stopped. The creek bed fell away beyond his sight.

Inching his way forward he realized that he was at the top
of a three hundred foot waterfall. The scant amount of water
spilling over clung to the sheer rock face. It was a straight shot to
the bottom of the vertical cliff, although the bottom was not in
view. To the East, an immense scree slope dropped steeply to the
floor below. On the West, vertical cliffs ended in a steeper scree
slope about one third of the way down.

"Hey, Willie," he shouted.

"What?"

"You gotta come here and look at this."

"What?" called the distant voice.

"Come here, ass hole."

Willie approached the brink with caution. Jay backed up
a little so that there was a place at the edge where Willie could
stand against the sidewall. Willie hesitated.

"Don't be such a faggot, Willie." Jay gave him more room
to advance along the safety of the sidewall, but Willie still

hesitated. The gentle gusts of wind channeled through the saddle in the rock tousled his curly hair. Willie grimaced, exposing a mouth full of braces.

"Look, Willie, if you piss in your pants, I won't tell anybody."

Anger flared across Willie's face. He pursed his lips, took a deep breath and stepped around Jay, moving slowly toward the precipice. When he reached the edge, he froze, his left hand glued to the vertical wall beside him, his right arm extended to his side as if to provide balance. He began to breathe in deep, rapid movements of his chest.

Jay watched him hyperventilate for a full minute, hoping he really would piss in his pants, just so he could tell everybody about it. Then it became boring. The boy just wasn't going to move.

Jay carefully approached Willie from the rear and gathered a fist full of Willie's purple jacket into his hand. As an afterthought, he realized that he might yet get Willie to piss his pants.

With a nudge of his fist, he said, casually, "Oops." Silently, Willie's center of balance moved beyond the edge of the waterfall. His arms held their frozen positions. Then Jay, with his muscular right arm, hauled back on Willie's purple nylon jacket. Willie's arms swung up and back as the sleeves of the unzipped jacket turned inside out. Jay stood, holding the empty jacket as he watched Willie float silently out of sight.

## SALT CREEK

Jay Vesco stood in the silence above the three hundred foot waterfall. A breeze gusted from the sun-warmed stone of the inner gorge. Three seconds passed before he heard a dull thud from below, merged into the sound of a small rock slide. He looked at the purple jacket in his right hand, trying to comprehend what had happened.

He advanced slowly toward the brink, then stood as Willie had stood, left hand on the rock wall, right arm poised to his side. His mind balked at looking straight down, not because of what he might see, but because of the seductive lure of unimpeded space.

The wall he touched with his left hand rose seven feet; above it, a scree slope continued upward, extending beyond the lip of the waterfall. Perhaps he could see the bottom from that vantage. He backed away from the edge, dropped the purple jacket at his feet, then turned and calmly walked twenty feet up the stone creek bed. From there, he mounted a steep scree slope to the West and shuffled along its lower margin. His traction was precarious on the fragments of shattered shale and sandstone.

*Need to climb higher.* Gradually, Jay crept his way up the shifting scree. His left foot rested against a fishhook cactus, which immediately broke free of its fragile roots and tumbled as a loose basketball, down the scree and into the creek bed, beside the purple jacket. Jay climbed as high and as close to the northern edge as he dared go. Crouching against the scree, he looked down. There, three hundred feet below, he saw the tiny body of Mr. T's son. From the disturbance of the scree far below, Jay thought Willie must have glanced off the steep slope, then slid the rest of the way.

*The worthless little fart should have zipped his jacket. And he definitely shouldn't have stood so close to the edge for so long.* Jay was confident that Willie would have eventually fallen off if he hadn't risked his own life to try to rescue him. *What a dumb shit. All Willie had to do was take one fucking little step backwards.*

Now, thought Jay, I'm stuck having to tell Mr. T that his little faggot son went and got himself killed. *It'll probably ruin the rest of the trip.* Jay began to shuffle back down the scree.

"Mr. T," Jay said aloud, "Willie just slipped and got killed." *That doesn't sound right.* He had not been down to the bottom himself. Willie might be just knocked out or something. "Mr. T, Willie fell and hurt himself." *That's the truth. He just could have hurt himself to death. Mr. T can go figure it out.*

Jay dropped into the creek bed and looked at the fishhook cactus and the jacket lying near the trickle of water. He picked up the jacket, then kicked the cactus far out beyond the brink of the waterfall. He didn't want it to land on Willie's head, in case he was alive.

As he stared at the purple nylon, shell jacket in his hand, he decided that it would be hard for Mr. T to really see that it was Willie's fault, if the jacket was up here. He wadded it up and tossed it over the edge.

Like a living thing, the purple jacket unfolded itself, extended its arms, then tumbled and soared in the warm breeze. For eight seconds, Jay watched the purple jacket ride the warm updraft, then glide out of sight.


Phil Thurman sat on a low boulder at Salt Creek Camp Ground. His bare feet had become a collage of tan and white mole skin, cut into circles, discs, strips and curves in an assortment of sizes, distributed randomly from the ankle bones to the toes. His feet hurt all over. But the discomfort of his feet was eclipsed by the throbbing of his wounded left hand.

He thought about Willie. Phil was frustrated and disappointed in the boy. He just never seemed to get things straight. Willie would never be able to respect himself until he built up his body. And hanging around with a skin and bones weakling like Davie wasn't helping matters. *A tall, skinny, bookworm Jew.* Phil just couldn't understand what his son saw in the awkward boy. It was true that Davie had his good points, like getting Willie through algebra. Willie did seem to gripe less when Davie was around. But he would never grow up until he spent more of his time with some solid, American kids like Jay.

"Do you know where Willie is, Mr. Thurman," asked Davie, who approached from above the campsite. "He said he would meet me up there to hunt for fossils." Davie pointed toward a slope to the Southwest.

"He's catching up on chores, Davie," Phil offered, cryptically.

"Oh." Davie scanned the area visible from the campsite.

"He went with Jay," Alicia volunteered, "to find some water." She pointed downstream.

"Thanks, Alicia."

"Here they are, now," Phil said as he watched Jay come into view.

Jay was jogging, empty handed, with his eyes to the gravel bed of the dry creek. Twenty yards from the campsite, he looked up and turned out of the creek, climbing the dirt trail to the campsite.

"Mr. T," said Jay, winded from the run, "Willie slipped and hurt himself. I think you better come."

Davie immediately turned in alarm toward the creek.

"Hold it! Hold it!" Phil shouted. "Is he able to walk?"

Jay looked at the ground.

"What exactly happened?" Phil asked, seeing a potential learning experience for Willie.

"I think you better come," Jay repeated.

"Is he hurt bad?" Phil asked.

Jay stammered. "Yeah...he just wouldn't listen."

With fear growing on Alicia's face, she pivoted and ran to the creek.

"Davie, go up that way," Phil pointed upstream, "and find Laura."

"But Willie's hurt," Davie said in near panic.

Phil stabbed his index finger in Davie's direction. "Go get Laura, then you can come down."

Phil Thurman watched briefly as Davie's long legs awkwardly vaulted him up one ledge then another until he vanished up the creek bed.

Phil jammed his bare feet into his boots, jerked and tied the laces, then ran down the creek with Jay following. Phil didn't know what to expect. Willie always tended to exaggerate things. *The boy is so melodramatic.* But Jay was always on the level.

They passed two stagnant pools, and eventually, a clear one with the water bottles lying about, some filled, some empty.

Phil looked to Jay for direction. Jay silently pointed downstream.

He found Alicia standing five feet from the lip of what was obviously an enormous drop. She stood motionless, both hands over her mouth, a wild stare in her eyes.

Phil turned to Jay. "Where is he?" he whispered. Fear gradually dissolved his irritation.

Jay pointed.

Phil could not get close enough to the edge to see Willie, but his heart sank. "Did you actually see him, Jay?"

"I had to climb up there." Jay pointed to the slope above them to the West.

Phil followed the scuff marks up the crumbling scree, his heart pounding with terror as he began to appreciate the magnitude of the cliff. He stretched his body full length across the tapering edge of the crumbled slope and looked over. A wave of dizziness swept over him, forcing him to close his eyes. When he opened them again, he saw the tiny immobile shape he knew to be his only son. His vision blurred with tears. Phil blinked them away and began to search for a way down. The wall to the East seemed to slope all the way to the bottom. It looked impossibly steep, but he saw only vertical cliffs in every other direction. He eased his way back over to the stone floor of the creek bed.

Alicia had not moved. Her hands remained at her mouth, the same wild stare in her eyes.

"Jay, take Alicia back to the campsite. And tell the others that I'm going to climb down that slope." He pointed to the eastern wall.

Phil sobbed as he circled back to approach the eastern slope that dropped to the bottom of the waterfall. He knew his son was dead. No one could survive a fall like that.

On reaching the top of the slope, Phil realized that it was even steeper than he had estimated. He placed a ten pound slab of rock firmly on the slope, then lifted his hands. The rock slid about 100 feet before stopping. The distant edge of the slope appeared to be not quite as steep, but he guessed that it would take at least fifteen minutes to traverse the top of the slope.

Laura, Jay and Davie appeared. Davie carried three walking sticks and packets of rope he had taken from each of their backpacks.

"Where is he, Daddy?" asked Laura.

Phil pointed toward the bottom. He could not see Willie from where he stood. Laura immediately began to traverse the upper edge of the scree slope, until she had advanced about thirty yards.

"Oh, my God," she cried. Laura returned.

Davie opened packets of rope, eighth-inch braided nylon rope.

"I'll go down," Davie said, "I'm the lightest one."

"You're not strong enough to carry him back up," Phil said, his hand unconsciously dismissing Davie.

"I can carry him, Dad," Laura pointed out, "besides, your hand is hurt."

"Sugar," Phil pronounced, "I already have one of my kids at the bottom of this canyon. So, you just stay put." Then turning to the football player, "Jay?"

Jay shook his head slowly from side to side. "Maybe we should get a helicopter or something."

Phil stared at Jay with disbelief and disgust. "What's all this rope supposed to do, Davie?" Phil asked.

"It won't hold your weight, but if you use it to keep from sliding, maybe you can get down," Davie said. "I don't know how you can get back up."

Phil picked up one of the polyethylene wrappers that the rope had been sold in. He read the back. "Davie, this says forty pound working load."

"It's all we have, Mr. Thurman," Davie answered. His voice was unsteady. "At the bottom of the chart it says the working load is six to fourteen percent of the tensile strength, so if you're careful, it should hold at least 286 pounds. I'm tying figure-of-eight follow through knots..." He swallowed a sob. "...so they won't weaken it as much."

Phil had never seen Davie use his head like this. "We've got to tie the top of it to something, Davie," he pointed out.

Through his despair, Phil watched as Davie took one end of the rope and wrapped it three times around the center of all three walking sticks. He tied the loose end back to the standing portion of the rope with a series of half hitches.

"We find a sturdy notch in the cliff up there," Davie explained, "and put the sticks behind it. Then somebody heavy sits on it."

"By God," said Phil, "I think that'll work. Sugar, you and your courageous friend take this up there and both of you sit on it. But pick a brace that's not gonna fall over on top of me."

Phil waited until Laura and Jay had anchored the rope in the cliff above, then proceeded to move out onto the slope.

"Mr. Thurman," yelled Davie, "I almost forgot." From the back of his waist band, Davie pulled out Phil's steerhide work gloves.

Phil edged back over to Davie and gratefully accepted the gloves. "You're thinking way ahead, Davie."

Out on the steep scree slope again, Phil made his way down in less than ten minutes, by occasionally stepping, but mostly sliding along the three hundred fifty feet of scree. The left glove was partially soaked through with blood from the puncture wound. Phil ignored the pain. He had reached the bottom.

He ran over to Willie, who was lying face up on the bottom edge of the opposite scree slope. He could see that Willie had struck the steep grade of the scree almost two hundred feet up, and had skidded to the bottom. He lay with his arms above his head, his eyes closed. There was some blood on the surrounding rocks, but not very much. Phil stood, with the tears in his eyes creating an illusion of movement. Phil blinked. He saw it again.

"Oh, dear God," he whispered, as he knelt over Willie. Willie was breathing. "Willie," he said, as he touched his son's smooth forehead. Willie did not stir. Phil placed his own cheek against Willie's and kept himself from crying.

Phil lifted himself up and turned toward Laura at the top to the slope. "He's alive!" He turned back to Willie and lifted his shirt. There were no signs of injury in front. He felt Willie's heart beating within his small chest. He must have landed on his back and skidded that way, thought Phil. He carefully moved Willie's head, revealing jagged cuts on his scalp. Turning Willie slightly sideways, he could see that the sweatshirt was shredded and that there were numerous cuts on his back, some deep, with small flaps of skin peeled upward, weeping blood. Willie's pants were ripped over the left buttock. There Phil found a five inch shard of stone stuck into the flesh. He pulled it out, starting fresh, bright red bleeding. The rock seemed to have stabbed its way between the muscle and the fat. Willie still did not stir.

Phil could not imagine how anyone could survive that fall, but for the moment, Willie was alive. Now he had to climb over three hundred feet of scree with Willie. What he could do for Willie at the campsite was a question that would have to wait.

He picked up the purple jacket lying nearby and tied it to Willie's waist. Using his pocket knife, he cut ten feet from the bottom end of Davie's climbing rope. With Willie's sweatshirt sleeves pulled up to his hands, Phil tied Willie's wrists together, using several wraps of the rope. He lifted Willie carefully and carried him to the opposite slope, the one he had descended. He lowered Willie's back gently onto the slope.

Phil removed his left glove. The crude bandage was soaked with new blood. The fingers worked, although flexing them produced pain. The thumb was nearly useless, since the cactus, which Davie had called an agave, had damaged the thick muscle at its base. Phil had descended the scree without relying on the strength of his left hand. To go back up, he would need both hands. He returned his hand to the glove.

Straddling his son, Phil inserted his head into the loop formed by Willie's arms. He knew that a person in shock should lie down, but Phil was unable to think of another way to get him up the slope. He would need both hands free. He tried to remember how a rope goes when you rappel. Although he had never learned to rappel, he could recall having watched it in some army recruiting add on TV. He passed the rope under his left arm, around his back, over his right hip and through his crotch. The trailing end then came under his right thigh and could be held by his right hand.

He began to climb, leaning into the slope, Willie's legs dragging between his own. With each cumbersome step, Phil took up the slack rope with his trailing right hand. After three minutes of exhausting effort, his thighs and calves ached with fatigue. For every two feet he climbed, the loose scree settled a foot. He looked back. The bottom of the slope was twenty feet below. It would take an hour to reach the top, if his strength lasted that long.

Davie's rope limited the slide after each step, but he was afraid to put too much weight on it. He and Willie together must weigh three hundred pounds. Phil decided to change the rope to the opposite side of his body, so that he could use the strength of his right arm to pull upward. He unwrapped himself from the rope.

The scree shifted beneath his feet. He fell to his left side, then onto his back, sliding to the bottom head first. With his son on top of him, Phil's only thought was to protect Willie's hands, which extended behind his own neck. He cruised over the sharp rocks with his back and head hunched forward, while he grasped Willie's sweatshirt near the shoulders.

His back screamed with pain from dozens of cuts. He accepted the pain. Willie may die regardless, but he knew Willie would surely die if he could not get him up the slope. Phil felt the back of his jacket: torn fabric and warm blood.

Laura's voice sounded from above, but he could not understand what she said. He waved one arm.

Beginning again, with the rope wrapped in the opposite direction, he climbed with his right hand high. The rope still didn't feel right. It cut into his back and the bottom of his left thigh. But with the added strength of his right arm, Phil eliminated much of the slippage. His muscles ached; his left hand drummed its rhythm of pain. Each step reached toward the boundaries of his endurance. Ten minutes had passed according to his wristwatch, much longer by the measure of his fatigue. He looked down. He was nearly a third of the way up the slope. A fall now would certainly break bones.

Phil struggled to the halfway point. The weight of Willie around his neck required him to call upon muscles seldom used. Phil thought of Willie's hands, tied together. He rested Willie against the slope and freed the arms from around his neck, allowing Willie's flaccid body to slide to the horizontal, stopping against Phil's legs.

Willie's hands were purple and white from lack of circulation. Still tied together, their color returned slowly as Willie's arms rested. The ashen color of Willie's face improved, marginally. Most of the bleeding had stopped.

Five minutes of rest restored Phil's strength, though his neck and back were still in spasm and his chest hurt. Looping Willie's arms around his neck, he climbed. Another five minutes, another fifty feet of slope, Phil Thurman could climb no higher. The pain in his chest increased. He held back tears. Phil raised his head against Willie's weight. "I can't," he shouted, "I can't make it." His eyes stung as sweat mingled with tears.

"Hold on to the rope, Dad," came Laura's voice from the cliff above.

His body felt lighter. The rope was moving, carving into his back and thigh, but it was tugging him upwards. He followed, one foot after the other. The constant pull from Willie's arms prevented him from looking up. Phil watched Willie's light brown curls punctuate each deep breath from his parched mouth. He was vaguely aware that, behind Willie's head, the crumbled shards of the slope were passing beneath them. The pain in his chest seemed to extend down his left arm.

Something caught his right arm. *A hand.* It was Laura, tugging him upward. Phil turned his head and realized that he had reached the top. Jay had been hauling the rope around his waist. Laura took Willie's arms from around Phil's neck and towed her brother, as gently as she could, to the level ground. Jay assisted Phil to the same spot, dragging the rope behind.

Davie knelt there, with three pack frames. The pack frames had been stripped of their bags, leaving cross-braced aluminum ladders. Two lay end to end, the third in the middle, overlapping both. Davie accepted the rope from Jay, then cut eight lengths of about ten feet each. With these he lashed the frames together. Phil watched, exhausted and preoccupied by the pain in his chest.

"Davie's making a stretcher," Laura explained, while untying her brother's hands.

"That's...good, Davie," Phil huffed. He removed his leather gloves. The left had taken on a veneer of dark brown blood and dirt. "I need some water."

Davie interrupted his lashing, unzipped his fanny pack and passed Phil the pint flask. Davie then completed the lashing. "This should work."

When Laura pulled Willie onto the makeshift stretcher, Davie looked at him for the first time, then touched Willie's forehead with a trembling hand. Phil silently shared the anguish, but could not cry.

Phil raised himself to his feet. Placing his hand on Davie's shoulder, he said, gently, "Let's get him back."

Davie stood and tied Willie to the stretcher. This done, they climbed their way back to the campsite, Jay at one end, Laura and Davie at the other. Phil collected the water bottles as they passed the clear pond. Those that were empty, he carried back empty. The pain in his chest subsided.


"Well, dammit!" Ranger Gluzack muttered, as he replaced the radio handset with obvious restraint. "I think the antenna's down."

"I'm not too surprised." Maria Sanchez had just confirmed that the phone lines from the BRO to the village and into the Canyon still didn't work. "At least the power's on."

"I've been able to pick up Flagstaff on the AM radio," Gluzack said. "The storm may not let up for another twenty four hours."

Sanchez knew that the Weather Service data were fed over the phone lines. The ice storm and subsequent blizzard had eliminated all two-way communication. Even the hand held radios depended on the relay antenna to reach into the Canyon, otherwise they functioned only in line-of-sight.

"If it's all right with you," said Sanchez, "I'll go down to Indian Garden tomorrow morning and relieve Mandi."

"Take a gun."

"You think Horn is down there?"

"I don't know where the hell he is. I don't know where the hell anybody is. For all I know, they caught him already. Just take a gun. Take that cannon."

"No problem." She knew that he was referring to her personal .357 magnum. She had qualified as "Expert" with the same gun back in San Antonio. "Because Bright Angel is so bad, I'm going to take a bunch of long crampons down for the Thurman party." They both were aware that the Thurman Party was the only party left in the backcountry, and were due to climb out the day after tomorrow. The short points of the crampons that she assumed the Thurman party carried would not be adequate for deep snow and ice, which now covered the upper trails.

"Tell Mandi to be careful climbing out."

"Special assignment when she gets back?" Maria asked.

"Yeah. Two ribeyes and a bottle of spätlese."

She smiled. "What should I tell her is for dessert?"

"Sweets."


David found he couldn't concentrate. He would be hyper for a while, then he couldn't move. Everything had come unglued.

Mr. Thurman sat slumped against a boulder, watching Laura and Alicia clean the wounds on Willie's head and back. Jay had made two trips down the creek for water.

Willie was still unconscious and pale. David sat on the ground beside him while the girls went off to wash out the towels they had used to bathe his wounds. David covered him with his sleeping bag. He knew the fall should have killed him. He admitted to himself that he expected Willie to die.

David pulled the sleeping bag toward Willie's head and noticed that his right foot was exposed. He pulled it up farther. His left leg appeared shorter than the right. Tossing the sleeping bag off Willie's legs, David compared the two legs. The left leg was shorter and rotated to the side. He unfastened Willie's waist cord and pulled the nylon pants and long johns down to the knees. David felt the right thigh. It felt normal. The left thigh muscle was thicker and knotted. As he moved the left leg, he felt the crepitus of grating bone fragments in the mid thigh. He covered Willie with the sleeping bag, got up, walked to the far side of a boulder and vomited.

When he had recovered, David took from his pack a zipper lock bag containing two books. He pulled out the larger book, NOLS Wilderness First Aid, and read the section on fractures. David went into his tent and brought out Willie's closed-cell foam sleeping pad. He wasn't sure about what to do with Willie's pants. He decided to splint the leg with the pants on, but as he was about to pull them up, he saw red appear, then blossom over the front of Willie's white briefs.

David turned to call Mr. Thurman, but saw that he was asleep. He lifted the briefs to find the wound, but realized that Willie had urinated the blood. He went to Willie's pack and returned with clean underpants and a small towel. He decided that he had better leave Willie's boot on for the splint. Using his pocket knife, he cut away the blood soaked underpants, wiped Willie clean with the new pair, folded the towel over him in place of underpants, and pulled up his pants. He poured water over the good underpants, squeezed them out, then tossed them through the door of his tent. This all felt like a bad dream—a very bad dream.

Using Willie's leg as a guide, David cut the foam pad with his knife. Doubling it over, he wrapped it around the leg and up the outside of the hip. This he tied in place with ropes on the leg and a leather belt at the waist. David consulted the book again.

The notion that he was simply completing a class project passed across his mind. *It definitely counts toward the final grade.* He tied his walking stick to the splinted leg and tightly to Willie's waist, placing more foam pad under the waist rope. The top of the stick, with its rope hand-loop, extended fifteen inches below Willie's boot. He made a rope harness for the boot, passed it through the loop on the stick, then pulled it tight, tying it firmly.

He looked at the traction splint. He didn't know if it was correct. He didn't really understand what it was supposed to do. But the book said that a broken femur needed one.

David looked inside Willie's pants again. There was no more blood. *People die from internal bleeding.* With the towel there, he would know if there was more. He looked up "abdominal injury" in the book, but found nothing that seemed to apply. *Only one first aid book.*

Willie's purple jacket caught David's attention. How had Willie's back been so badly cut without cuts, or even blood, on the jacket? He examined the jacket. It was turned inside out. He found a tiny apple-shaped wooden Christmas ornament in one of the pockets. He remembered with a chill of horror the scene at Santa Maria Spring, the first day. Jay had grasped Willie's jacket and pushed him over the edge, pulling him back with the jacket. David was startled to find Jay standing above him, also gazing at the jacket. David turned the purple jacket right-side out and covered Willie.

## INDIAN GARDEN

Jeffrey Horn stood with his back to the railing of Plateau Point. He had followed the trail away from Indian Garden, and now knew that he would have to go back. Wider than the footpaths he had traveled for four days, this trail would allow three hikers to walk abreast. He saw unmistakable signs of heavy use, by both hikers and mules. Horn had risked the relatively flat, uninterrupted terrain, devoid of cover, in the hope that it would lead him to the bridge that spanned the Colorado river. He was mentally prepared to endure the wilderness and deep snow of the Arizona Strip, beyond the North Rim, and survive. But the way to the bridge eluded him. Without a map, he had resigned himself to following his intuition in choosing which trail to walk, and in which direction.

Behind him, the dead end of the Plateau Point trail was marked by the railing of an overlook. He peered over the rail again. Thirteen hundred feet below, trapped within massive walls of black stone, the river continued its endless carving of the Canyon. It was obvious to him that there was no way to climb down.

Over the past three days, he had become accustomed to the abrupt disappointments of the Canyon. A gentle creek bed would descend promisingly along a geologic fault, allowing him passage through the crumbled remnants of one cliff, only to halt him on the verge of a fifty foot plummet at the next. A shortcut across the head of a minor side-canyon had often required of him the same time, and twice the effort as following the meandering trail around its margin. His intuition had proven worthless.

Ledges that had appeared from a distance to be separated by a ten foot slope would expand on his approach, leaving him in frustration at cliffs separated by thirty feet of unscalable scree.

His only good fortune seemed to be the storm over the South Rim. The light drizzle falling about him must be burying the Rim in snow or ice. That could account for the absence of tourists and hikers. It might also offer him, he hoped, an opportunity to climb out to the South Rim, if he could not locate the bridge soon.

Horn's problem for the moment was the need to approach Indian Garden and locate a trail that would lead him into the inner gorge. That, he knew, would be the trail to the bridge. He saw a deep side canyon just to the East and a long canyon across from it, north of the river. The bridge must be there, he thought. The trail leading to the bridge should be wide and show signs of the mules that, he knew, traveled between the Rim and Phantom Ranch at the bottom.

Staff Sergeant Jeffrey Horn reprimanded himself for his self indulgence. He realized that he should not have paused this long in the open. Although he was confident that he could not be observed by binoculars from the cloud-encased Rim, there were countless hiding places all about him that could allow his pursuers to observe his movements. He stood erect, hefted his sack of food and gear, then took one last look into the yawning gorge. Mindful of possible observers, he confidently headed back toward Indian Garden.

As he passed the intersection with the trail from which he had emerged earlier, he longed for the sense of comfortable isolation that he had enjoyed for two days along the narrow footpath. The broad avenue on which he now traveled threatened him with the greater probability of encountering those who might recognize him, seize him, and imprison him.

One man had died during his escape, though Horn knew he was not at fault. Would he kill to remain free? He had no ready answer.

Indian Garden, the sign promised him, would have water and toilets. Water, he had obtained without difficulty in the side canyons of the Tonto Trail. He doubted that he would have been so fortunate in Summer. Toilets, however, held a special meaning in a tourist area. Unlike the occasional wilderness latrines he had found along the Tonto, this one, he knew, would have toilet paper. The desert of the Canyon provided him few suitable substitutes. Acquiring toilet paper, he concluded, might be worth some risk.

Horn left the deserted trail when he reached the shrubs and trees of Indian Garden. There he found the eastern continuation of the Tonto Trail, which, according to the sign, would connect him with the trail to the bridge. He saw no hikers or rangers on any of the trails, or at Indian Garden. He decided to go for the toilet paper, then for the bridge. Keeping to the line of shrubs and gullies by the creek, he headed toward a two-story brown structure, from which protruded four rooftop ventilation stacks. Even though it was December, he observed that the surrounding cottonwood trees still bore yellowing leaves, as did most of the low shrubs. After days on the Tonto, this struck Horn as a verdant oasis.

During his frequent pauses, he observed no movement in the campground. Approaching the building that he assumed to be the latrine, he took note of an empty mule corral, and about a hundred yards away, the ranger station. Still no sign of movement. He proceeded carefully past the front of the latrine and climbed the steps to the deck. He listened. He heard no sounds coming from behind the stall doors. He opened the first door with a touch of his hand. Inside, he found the toilet paper dispenser empty. The back of the door was posted with a sign describing for him the unique functioning of the solar powered, self-composting toilet. Indeed, the air within the fully enclosed stall smelled pleasant. He hoped one of the stalls would still have enough toilet paper to make the side trip worth it.

SSgt. Horn opened the door and looked into the unflinching face of a solidly built Navajo man wearing the uniform of a Park Service ranger.

"Uh..." Horn's mind raced. "Out of paper. It's out of toilet paper," he said with a feeble smile, unable to convince even himself. "Guess I'll try the next one." The ranger's eye contact was not casual, thought Horn. Those were the eyes a predator presents to its prey. He knew the ranger had identified him.

"Drop your bag and turn around, please sir, and put your hands against the wall."

Horn tossed the bag onto the deck. As he turned to the wall, he realized that the ranger had no weapon. Though Horn had not been to his dojo in fifteen months, he felt certain about the outcome of this encounter. Despite the Navajo's massive arms, bull neck and dominating confidence, Horn knew he could take him down, then flee. His heart pounded.

The ranger nudged Horn's feet away from the wall, then patted him down. "You don't look much like your picture, Sergeant Horn." Horn's right arm was then seized and twisted behind him. Pain tore at his shoulder.

Jeffrey Horn ignored the pain and waited to be turned away from the wall. As soon as the front was clear, he snapped forward, grabbing the ranger's right coat sleeve with his hammer-locked right hand. In one fluid motion he rotated his torso to the right, turning the big Navajo away. The follow-through of his left hand pounded the corner of his fist into a pressure point beneath the ranger's right ear. With a grunt and one step away from Horn, the ranger threw both of his tree trunk arms into Horn, spinning him and slamming him against the wall again. Within one second the ranger had trapped Horn in a full Nelson, by reaching under both of Horn's arms and locking his hands behind Horn's neck.

The Navajo fought with remarkable strength, Horn lamented. The pressure point hit should have dropped him. *It was a good hit.* Horn shifted his hips to the left, allowing his leg to sweep behind the ranger's knee. They both dropped to the deck.

With a deft roll, the Navajo was on top. Horn quickly reached his left arm around the ranger's neck and grabbed a fist full of dense black hair from behind the opposite ear. With a forceful yank, the ranger's head torqued his body away from Horn.

They both rolled to their feet. Horn now knew that he could not match the strength of this Navajo ranger. He would have to end the fight.

As the ranger drove a powerful right, roundhouse punch toward his face, Horn deflected the blow by crossing his right arm under the left, feinting to the left, and striking the pressure point below the back of the ranger's right elbow. Completing the flourish, both of Horn's crossed hands simultaneously struck the ranger's head at the left temple and right chin, violently twisting the ranger's head diagonally.

The Navajo dropped to the deck, arms and legs in spasm. Horn had not wanted to kill him, but this powerful, self-assured man would not go down any other way.

Horn opened the second stall door. He saw toilet paper in the holder. He unwound a stack of it, then sat down on the closed stool lid. His chin quivered. He had just killed a man for toilet paper. Why had the ranger forced him to that extreme? SSgt. Horn felt anger. That, and an icy wave of fear in his stomach. This is all so crazy. He wiped his nose on his jacket sleeve, then looked at the dark blood stains left from the car wreck.

He pressed his eyelids together tightly. There, in the darkness, he sees the camo covered face again.

*"What's the matter with you?" it shouts in his memory, "It's just a game!"*

He opened his eyes and the filtered light of the stall returned.

He would take the ranger's heavy uniform coat. It would be warmer. It might also provide some disguise at a distance, he thought. *And money.* He might need money over the next few weeks. He stuffed the toilet paper into his shirt pocket and stood to leave.

The light changed. The stall door was opening toward him. Horn leaned away from the opening. A .38 service revolver appeared, held by a hand with a green sleeve. With all his strength, SSgt. Horn slammed the door, trapping the hand at the wrist. The gun fired, then clattered to the floor. Horn snatched up the gun, flung the door open, and squeezed the trigger, firing it point blank, into the face of a ranger.

The ranger, much smaller than the Navajo, toppled backwards onto the deck. *Breasts.* He realized it was a petite woman. Placing the gun into his belt with a trembling hand, Horn stepped out of the stall to look at her—another death. She had been a beautiful woman with short blond hair, the sort of ranger, he thought, who teaches children about pine trees and lizards. Now he watched blood pump rhythmically out of the fatal wound in her forehead. It poured onto the deck and spilled through the gaps between the wooden planks.

Jeffrey Horn considered the price of this needless side trip. A surge of grief briefly touched him, as he took the wallet and coat from the dead Navajo. He did not look again at what he had done to the young woman.

Since no one responded to the sound of the gunshots, he assumed that these two were the only staff at Indian Garden.

Horn took his sack and, still watchful, hurried away from Indian Garden.

David Cadranel sat inside his tent, in the dark. Willie lay beside him. The door was still open, allowing David to stare into the darkness of Salt Creek campsite. Now wrapped in a sleeping bag, Willie remained unconscious, with nauseous wounds all over his back, internal bleeding, and at least a broken femur. David could see Mr. Thurman's silhouette against a boulder.

David wished that someone here knew what to do to help Willie. But after the others had seen the traction splint, everyone, including Mr. Thurman, deferred to David's judgment. He felt crushed beneath the burden of Willie's life or death. What did he know? He had read a first aid book and had practiced none of it.

Willie's injuries, he believed, would have doctors rushing about, giving urgent orders and consulting specialists and X-rays and blood tests. There would be beeping machines and a flurry of nurses.

Earlier, he had tried to put a few drops of water into Willie's mouth, but Willie didn't swallow. Every few minutes since then, he wet his finger and dabbed it onto Willie's dry lips. He hoped that Willie had filled his stomach with water before he fell. David had read about the dangers of dehydration in the Canyon. He held no hope that Willie could survive.

That afternoon he had read about signals, in Elements of Survival, but no planes flew over, no other hikers came by, and the upper canyon was shrouded in dense, gray clouds. He gave up on the idea. Willie was right. It is a stupid little book. They would have to carry Willie to the ranger station at Indian Garden. That would be a long, slow walk carrying a stretcher. Mr. Thurman had said he would continue alone to Indian Garden when they reached the Horn Creek campsite.

The light drizzle was hardly noticeable. Rocky ground soaked it up as it landed. Only the fly of each tent showed signs of the dampness by loosening and wrinkling a bit.

David inserted his hand into Willie's sleeping bag and felt inside his nylon pants. The towel he had placed there was still dry. He slid his hand over to Willie's hand and held it. With his other hand, David replaced a small stuffed rabbit that had slipped from beneath Willie's arm, which lay across his chest. Willie breathed in long, slow sighs.

He placed the palm of Willie's hand against his own. The skin was smooth and cool. It had no life in it, no warmth. Fingernails were uneven, cracked in places along the margins. Willie's fingers folded without resistance. The knuckles were not bony like his own. The palm had more flesh, was more supple. David brought Willie's fingers to his lips and held them there, willing him to live.

He tucked the hand beneath the warmth of the sleeping bag and sat for what seemed like an hour, struggling against a wave of desperate isolation. He wondered if Willie would be alive in the morning. These might be Willie's last hours of life, yet he was unaware that David was there.

With a fingertip, David felt the contour of Willie's eyebrows in the darkness. They gently bristled in one direction, lay flat in the other. His closed eye was firm, like a liquid filled ball, beneath its loosely draped eyelid. The nose was hard at the top, flexible and resilient toward the tip. Willie's lips yielded to the light pressure of his fingertip. He could feel the little dip in the center, as Willie's warm breath played on his fingertips.

Mr. Thurman's cigarette lighter flared. In the light, David could see a scorpion on the ground near Mr. Thurman's foot. Mr. Thurman lit a cigarette, turned up the flame on the butane lighter, then reached down with it and immolated the fleeing scorpion.

## HORN CREEK

Maria Sanchez leaned into the driving snow as she fought her way across the deep accumulation on the parking lot near the Bright Angel Trail head. She knew that the sun must have risen already, but its light only lent a lighter cast to the drifting haze that tore at her face. A foot of new snow had fallen during the night and promised to continue through the morning. The layered snow and ice of the previous day had made it nearly impossible for snow plows to find enough traction to push their way along the roads of Grand Canyon Village. Sanchez assumed they would try again this morning with full chains. Perhaps that would bring a little activity back to the deserted roads and businesses.

She stepped confidently through the deep snow, using a ski pole as a walking stick, the same one she used even in the summer. To the bottoms of her boots were lashed the twelve-point crampons she had pulled from the deepest corner of her foot locker this morning. She had never imagined that there would be a use for them at Grand Canyon. But this was a storm of rare severity. Her usual four-point instep crampons did not seem adequate for the steep, ice and snow covered trails that she expected to find for at least the first two hundred vertical feet. It would be difficult enough just to avoid walking off the trail in the present white out. The more vertical surfaces, she hoped, would still show areas of exposed rock to provide visual orientation. She began her descent along the deserted trail.

In addition to the usual change of clothes and odd supplies, she had also placed in her pack six sets of long spike instep crampons for the Thurman party. They were due to climb out tomorrow.

She reached the first tunnel of the upper trail. To her surprise, the snow and ice extended the full length of the tunnel.

She would try to make it down to Indian Garden before noon. She hoped that would allow Mandi Fisher time to make it back up for her ribeye dinner and dessert with Gluzack. She liked Mandi, who had been an interpretive ranger at the Park for the last year. Mandi's enthusiasm apparently had not yet been tainted by the police and crowd control duties that, she knew, had turned off so many young rangers. And despite Gluzack's frequent grumbling about how the Boy Scouts and the Sierra Club thought they owned the place, Mandi still seemed to enjoy working with the Boy Scout groups that frequently hiked the Canyon. Of course, she was aware that Mandi's father had been a Scoutmaster for many years. That probably accounted for the twinkle Sanchez always saw in Mandi's eyes whenever the young ranger sat with a group of Scouts to talk about where they had been and what they had planned for the future.

Sanchez looked out into the Canyon. She saw nothing but white, driving snow. She should be nearing the top of the Coconino. She had never seen such heavy snow this far down, nearly five hundred vertical feet. Starting into the precipitous switchbacks of the Coconino, her gait began to feel like that of an Arctic hiker, testing the way with her ski pole, then digging in the heel of the crampon with each step. She cringed at the thought of negotiating this with only instep crampons.


For David, the night had been unending. He had tried to stay awake, but had repeatedly caught himself dozing. Each time, he would reprimand himself, while hurriedly checking on Willie, who was unchanged, even now. The intermittent drizzle had eventually prompted him to close the tent door, eliminating the chill breeze that had served to awaken him.

It was daylight. Willie was alive. Beyond those two facts, his fatigued brain was incapable of analysis. His back and neck ached from sleeping in various unnatural positions. The night, David decided, had been more exhausting than the Hermit Trail and the night climb down the inner gorge. It had been the worst night of his life, and it was over.

He opened the tent, walked to the far side of a boulder and peed. As he returned, Mr. Thurman emerged from the light blue tent. The man had aged overnight. Great, dark bags hung below his bloodshot eyes. His thick arms drooped limply from sagging shoulders. His gait was more of a rocking shuffle, with all the energy gone out. The crude bandage on his left hand was partially displaced, held together by brown crust. He looked at David from a lax, ashen face.

"How is he, Davie?"

"About the same."

"Did he wake up?"

"No."

"What do you think?"

"I don't know." David shook his head. "I'll get everybody up."

"Good." Mr. Thurman wandered to the latrine.

After breakfast, prepared by Laura and Alicia, they struck camp and, with little conversation, mounted the trail to Indian Garden. The gray sky and gray-green shale echoed David's somber mood.

To David, fossils and geologic formations had lost their relevance. The slopes and cliffs had merged in his mind into a single, dreadful barrier that separated Willie from the help that might save his life. The weight on his back had become one with the burden in his heart. Hope seemed as inaccessible as the clouds beyond the massive Redwall. The dirge of footfalls crunching onto the narrow trail carried him forward.

The plan was to walk to Horn Creek. According to the map, the two campsites were one mile apart. He couldn't say, one mile "as the crow flies," since even a bird would have to fly around or over Dana Butte, which towered between. By the arithmetic of the Grand Canyon, he knew the distance was over three miles of tortuous Tonto Trail, hugging the cliffs above the inner gorge for the first third.

Since Willie's stretcher was made of three pack frames, they had needed to redistribute their packs' contents. Alicia's pack was nearly empty anyway, so she carried her sleeping bag and a few other items in a stuff sack. Laura's things went to Mr. Thurman, with Jay carrying the extra sleeping bag tied to his pack. David carried everything of Willie's.

"The stretcher's coming apart again," Laura said.

"I'll get it," David replied.

"Show me how you do it," Laura suggested, "then it won't take so much time."

David explained the lashing to her as he retied one.  He watched as Laura retied the others.  The litter bearers rotated and continued on the trail.  David felt only despair.

With rest breaks every fifteen minutes, the hike to Horn creek required four hours.  As they entered the canyon of Horn Creek, David noticed, at the top of the Redwall, a series of cave openings, situated above five hundred feet of sheer cliff.  Two caves were lower, one appearing to be about a hundred feet up, at the back of the side canyon, the other, thirty feet above a long and steep scree slope.  Indians, he thought, must have gone up to the lowest one at some time.

David had read that the ancient Indians, perhaps the ancestors of the Hopi, had made the Canyon their home for thousands of years.  They had built stone houses and made baskets, pottery and wooden figurines.  He knew that artifacts had been found in practically every side canyon and on top of the highest buttes and temples.   The accessible caves were supposedly used as granaries or for ceremonies, or possibly for defense.  David considered it nothing less than awesome that, before King David built the Temple in Jerusalem, ancient Indians had already placed split-twig figurines of deer into the limestone caves of the Redwall.  But these ancient ones had disappeared from the Canyon eight hundred years ago.  With Willie dying, none of these profound revelations from David's books seemed as important as when he had read them.

Passing the western branch of Horn Creek, David looked down into the drainage.  Butchart's little book had described a way down to the river by following the base of the Tapeats from here.  It looked more difficult than the trail they had descended three nights before, with Willie in the lead.  He couldn't imagine why anyone would try to get down to the river that way, unless the creeks were dry.  While he saw no water flowing where the Tonto Trail crossed the western fork of Horn Creek, he was confident, from having found water in the last two side canyons, that it would only require walking down the creek bed until reaching a rock layer that prevented the water from seeping into the ground.  Besides, there had been a light drizzle all morning.  Precipitation that fell on the upper canyon, he knew, would have to end up down here.

Along the Tonto, the creeks seemed to appear from nowhere, at the top of the Bright Angel, but were often buried beneath slopes of accumulated debris. He had found the water that trickled down the creek beds waiting in basins and catch pockets of the eroded Tapeats before it seeped into the stone. *A lot of good the water is if Willie can't swallow.*

They hiked the remaining quarter mile to the tiny campsite along the sloped bank of Horn Creek's eastern branch. David was exhausted from a night of sitting awake beside Willie. He immediately pitched his tent beneath the shelter of a small stand of desert willow and mesquite, so that Willie could be placed out of the drizzle.

After resting for fifteen minutes and eating lunch, Mr. Thurman announced, "I'm going on to Indian Garden and get some help."

"Why don't we all just go there, Dad?" Laura asked.

"I don't know about you guys, but I can't carry Willie any farther today," he answered. There was resignation in his voice.

"I can't either," added Jay.

"It shouldn't be more than about two or three hours, round trip," Mr. Thurman continued.

"I'll go with you, Mr. T," Jay said tentatively. He seemed uncomfortable around David, and they both knew why.

"No. I want you to stay together, and to stay here." A shadow of uncertainty seemed to creep into Mr. Thurman's voice. To David, Mr. Thurman looked like somebody with the flu. He moved so sluggishly and his face was so pale. David suspected from the swelling at Mr. Thurman's left wrist that his injured hand had become infected.

Mr. Thurman took a quart bottle of water. Before leaving, he walked over to Willie's tent, knelt there with his hand on Willie's forehead for a few moments, then climbed the slope above the campsite and slowly walked off toward Indian Garden.

Soon Jay wandered off toward the West. Laura rummaged through the first aid kit for anything that might help Alicia's infected ankle. Depression and fatigue were evident in all their faces.

David sat in a daze beside Willie. He heard a soft moan. Willie's face was contorted in a grimace of pain.

"Laura," David called, "Willie's waking up."

Laura ran to the tent. "Willie," she said.

There was no response. His eyes remained closed in a frozen image of pain.

"Water," David demanded suddenly, "get me a water bottle."

Maybe Willie could swallow, he thought. When Laura returned with a quart bottle, David opened it and poured a few drops through Willie's clenched teeth. Willie gagged and coughed it out.

"Swallow, Willie," he said.

He poured a few more drops. Willie gagged again, and coughed it out. David began to cry.

"Swallow it, Willie," he shouted.

He tried again. Willie swallowed and coughed.

"He's going to choke," Laura cautioned. "Maybe you shouldn't do that anymore, Davie."

"He hasn't peed since yesterday," he retorted, now crying uncontrollably. "He's got to drink. He's got to."

Laura walked away.

"Willie, it's David. You've got to drink." He poured a little water. Willie coughed it out. "You've got to drink, or you'll die. Willie, swallow the water. Swallow the water."


Maria Sanchez walked past the deserted campground at Indian Garden. She had capped her crampons and stowed them in her pack when she paused at Mile-and-a-half Rest House, below the Coconino. The trail here was dry, even though it was drizzling. She headed directly for the ranger station.

Entering the front door, she dropped her pack on a chair and walked to the back.

"Anybody home?" There was no answer. "Mandi," she called.

She noticed the desk drawer wide open. Looking inside it, she was chilled by the realization that the .38 revolver had been removed from its holster. She leaned over the desk and looked out the corner windows. Nothing stirred. She knew Mandi was not a person to rely on a gun. The girl could barely shoot the thing.

Sanchez drew her .357 magnum from its holster on her side, checked to be certain it was fully loaded, then headed out the door. When she reached a picnic table, she knelt and looked about carefully at the shrubs and the cottonwoods, the mule corral and the latrine. Nothing moved.

She walked in a crouch to the corral, then over to the benches below the latrine. Still crouching, she looked up and down the trail. Slowly, she climbed the stairs to the latrine deck.

There she saw the two rangers sprawled on the deck.

Maria Sanchez felt a chill sweep from her face to her feet, then burning warmth over her ears. A bitter taste rose in the back of her mouth, as her stomach tightened. She could feel her heart pounding, see her vision throb with every beat. She could not see who these rangers were, but she knew. The deck before her, took on a surrealism that allowed her to separate herself and her decisions from the dark blood and foraging insects. She forced her mind to formulate a plan, a course of action that set aside the horror.

Starting at the first stall door, she squatted, then eased the door open, her gun leveled and held well away from the door. She repeated this silently at each stall. From the vantage of the deck, she scanned the horizon again. No one was visible.

Sanchez stooped over Jonathan Grey Sky. His neck was broken. His wallet was gone. And so was his coat, she realized.

She went over to Mandi Fisher. A bullet hole had penetrated her forehead just above the center of her left eyebrow. Her gun was nowhere around.

Forcing back her emotions, she judged from the position of Mandi's body, that the fatal shot had been fired from inside the second stall. She opened the door again and examined the floor and the walls. In the back wall she found a bullet hole. She shook her head.

Gluzack had been wrong, and both Mandi and Grey Sky had paid. She realized that she alone now knew that Sergeant Horn had not headed west.

"Oh, God," she mumbled aloud, as she thought of the Thurman party. *They must have crossed paths.*

She looked at the two bodies a moment longer, then ran back to the ranger station. She tried the phone to the Rim. It was still out. She checked the desk drawer. The .38 caliber ammo box was still there. *The bastard has four more shots.*

Sanchez pondered the situation for a moment, unwilling to allow the emotion of it paralyze her, then grabbed a pair of hand cuffs and their key. She headed to the door, then stopped and returned to the back office. From the top of the bookcase, she lifted a pair of binoculars, pulling them from their nylon case and draping the strap around her neck. Although she carried no more ammunition for her own gun, she was confident that, if she needed to use it, one shot would do the job.

Walking out of the station and toward the trail to the North, she considered the prospect of confronting an armed killer along the Tonto Trail.


Jeffrey Horn knew now that he should have continued up to the Rim from Indian Garden, yesterday. The storm would have been perfect. New snow would have covered his tracks. He would have been out of this cursed canyon. It would not let go of him.
He recalled, with frustration, his poor decisions of the previous day. He had descended the Bright Angel Trail into the inner gorge yesterday, and had reached the silver bridge. But armed rangers waited on the north bank. When darkness approached, they had turned lights onto the bridge and onto the approach from a second bridge a half mile upstream. He had waited most of the night, but had seen no opportunity to get across. Before dawn, he had climbed back out of the inner gorge, the way he had come.

At the top of the gorge, he had located a secluded niche in which to sleep. On awakening, near mid day, he had made the belated decision to climb out to the Rim. However, after passing above Indian Garden, he had once again turned himself around at the sight of movement on the trail near the base of the Redwall. The thought of confronting, and possibly killing, another ranger softened his will. He had moved quickly back through Indian Garden and headed west again on the Tonto.

As he walked now along the narrow undulating trail, reflecting on these poor decisions and his hopeless predicament, Horn cleared a rise and saw, twenty yards away, a man seated on a rock, clumsily untying his boot. Horn backed away, unseen. He walked rapidly east for a hundred yards, until he remembered what lay in that direction. He paused, then walked over to the nearby cliff, which dropped into the gorge.

He closed his eyes.

*He sees the Cascade Mountains. He is the hunter, one of the "Goons," as they are labeled by the students of the survival course. The pairs of students are to avoid capture by practicing their evasion skills. He is to track them down and capture them. He and the other instructors wear black uniforms to set a mood of fear in the students. He comes upon two careless students sitting in a small clearing, one facing away, the other untying his boot. Both are wearing mud-encrusted flight suits.*

*"On the ground, American Pigs!" he shouts, wielding his empty AK-47.*

*They both look up with shock, their faces amateurishly decorated with camo makeup.*

Horn opened his eyes and gazed again into the inner gorge of the Grand Canyon. He had only three choices, as he saw it. He could surrender himself and face life in prison or death. He could go on running, which would certainly mean more killing, or he could take ten steps forward and put a stop to the madness. All three choices seemed likely to end in his own death.

The question was how long would he struggle before he died. What life could he possible live if he did escape? He regretted catching himself when he slipped on the icy trail so many awful days ago.

He felt the gun tucked into his belt. He looked at the green coat he had stolen from the dead Navajo. It could end here. He took two tentative steps toward the Tapeats cliff. He was breathing rapidly. It was the only choice. The outcome would be the same. Staff Sergeant Jeffrey Horn gathered his strength. The Canyon had, at last, become his friend.

"Thank God, I found you." The voice came from behind.

Horn spun around.

"We need your help," said the middle aged man, with anguish in his voice, pain in his gait, and an unworldly ashen color to his face.

Horn watched as the man approached.

"It's my son. I'm Phil Thurman. My son, Willie, fell. He's hurt really bad."

*Willie Thurman.* The name chimed in his memory, bringing the shadowed image of the curly haired, blue eyed boy who had climbed down to the rapids in the dark, just to take a picture. His tall, skinny friend had given him a canteen and the tablets. "What happened?" His voice was coarse from disuse.

"He fell off a cliff," he pointed west, "back at Salt Creek. He's been unconscious since yesterday. And I think his leg is broken." He panted to catch his breath. "Today we carried him to Horn."

"What?"

"We carried him to Horn Creek. Should we have stayed at Salt?"

Horn Creek, he thought. *They carried him to Horn.* Did he really owe the boy anything? He thought not. But his father looked like walking death. Horn doubted that the man would make it to get help. "Let's...uh...let's go to Indian Garden," Horn stammered, finding the words incredible, "and we can call on the phone for help."

"Bless you, Ranger...Grey Sky is it?"

Horn stared blankly, then noticed, for the first time, the name tag on the green coat. "Yeah." With his left arm he assisted Phil Thurman, and turned east onto the Tonto trail.

"Freeze," shouted a woman in green, standing ten yards in front of him. She aimed a revolver with one hand and supported it in the other.

Jeffrey Horn had been ready to die, but he was not ready to be killed. With Thurman partly blocking his body, Horn drew his gun and took careful aim. She must be afraid of hitting Thurman, he thought. Horn fired.

The woman in green folded at the waist, stumbled backwards five steps and disappeared over the Tapeats cliff.

Thurman, with terror on his face, backed away from Horn. His hand clutched at his chest. The terror in his expression changed to surprise and pain. He was as white as a dead man.

"No!" Horn yelled, "Don't..."

Phil Thurman spun to flee. His first faltering step carried him off the Tapeats in the very spot that Horn had chosen for himself. Thurman fell with only a strangled moan.

Horn stood, stunned by the inescapable cascade of horror. The end of all this madness had seemed so close. Instead, it had fed upon itself and grown hungrier. He would hurt no one, he thought, if he could just be somewhere far away from here.

He walked over to where Phil Thurman had fallen from the cliff. On a rock shelf one hundred feet below, Thurman's body lay in an impossible contortion. He thought of the boy with the curly hair. There was nothing he could do about that now.

Horn walked to the cliff where the ranger had fallen. Fifteen feet below, the woman lay face down on an outcrop of rock.

"I'm sorry," he said aloud to her back. "I didn't want all this to happen. I didn't want anyone to die. Why were you there?" If she had not pointed the gun, he thought, if she had just allowed him to surrender, if she had just said, "Put your gun down and no one else will get hurt," it would have ended differently. He was sure.

Jeffrey Horn returned to the trail. He looked East and considered what waited for him there. He turned and looked West. He would find the curly haired boy, whom he could no longer help. He sat on a slab of rock by the trail and put his face into his hands.


David looked over the remnants of the first aid kit using his flashlight. Alicia's right ankle had become red and swollen, and she now complained of pain in her right groin. David saw that there was no more of the brown ointment for cuts. The first aid kit contained only useless junk, plus six acetaminophen tablets in separate little packets.

"I don't know what to do, Alicia," David said in despair.

"I think it needs like an antibiotic or something," Laura suggested.

That sounded good to David, but the nearest doctor was four thousand feet up the Canyon wall.

"I have an antibiotic," Jay offered.

David, Laura and Alicia all turned their eyes to Jay, waiting for further explanation of his unlikely possession.

"For my zits," he said, pointing one finger at a possible target on his left cheek.

"We need the kind you swallow," Laura said with disappointment.

"Erythromycin 250," he clarified, with a smile of victory. Jay got up, opened a side pocket of his pack, and returned with a plastic 35mm film container. Inside, David saw six round, orange horse pills.

"How much do you take?" David asked.

"One a day.  But when I first started them, last year, it was four times a day."

"How do you know it's the right one?" asked Alicia.

"That's easy," David replied, "It's the only one."

"I guess it can't make things worse," Alicia said.  David detected no relief in her voice.

"It used to make me puke, if I took it on an empty stomach," Jay added.

"You're just trying to make it sound good, so you can raise the price," Alicia quipped.

Jay tossed the container to her.

Alicia consumed a granola bar, followed by one of the orange pills and a gulp of water.  "If I puke, it's on your hands," she said with sincerity.

Jay looked at his hands.  The four of them managed a feeble laugh.

David returned to his tent.  Willie had never awakened enough for David to say that he really woke up.  But during those times when he had stirred and was aware of his pain, David had managed to get him to swallow, over dozens of attempts, maybe a pint of water.  Willie was out now.  He checked the towel in Willie's pants.  His spirits lifted.  The towel was damp in the middle.  He turned on his flashlight and looked at the underside of the beige towel.  There was only a trace of a red ring.  He felt it.  It was definitely wet in the center.  His bleeding must have slowed, or stopped, he thought.

He got out a small, yellow towel of his own, and put it where the beige one had been.  Outside the tent he looked again at the wet spot on the towel.  It wasn't much, but it was progress.  He poured some water on it, then squeezed it out.  Inside the tent he hung it to dry.

Willie probably needed an antibiotic too, for all the deep cuts on his back.  He and Laura had washed Willie's back again that afternoon with boiled water.  The wounds looked terrible to him. David knew he would have to content himself with a little water in, a little water out.

The others had stopped talking.  David assumed they had gone to sleep.  By then Willie had aroused enough to take a few more sputtering, unconscious swallows.  David wondered what they would do if Willie woke up completely.  The pain must be unbearable. Maybe the acetaminophen would help some, but he doubted that.

Earlier, they had discussed Mr. Thurman's delay in returning with help. They had agreed to wait until morning. If he hadn't returned by then, they would have to walk out, with Willie on the makeshift stretcher.

Something moved in the darkness outside the tent. David froze where he sat, by the open door of his tent. His eyes strained to see in the dark. Again he saw something move. Beneath the single sack of food hanging from a tree branch he saw two white wraiths circling rapidly. He watched in amazement. They moved up the slope, then returned, like a dust devil, never stopping, never assuming corporeal form in his eyes.

Perhaps fatigue was causing his mind to invent these wisps of constant movement. He looked away, but they did not follow his gaze. Something was there, circling beneath the food, hovering about the backpacks, and returning to the food.

With the patience of a tiger lily opening at dawn, David reached for his flashlight and aimed the dark cylinder toward the wraiths. He switched it on. In the instant before they fled, he saw two slender, catlike animals with vertical, foot long tails, ringed with alternating bands of black and white.

He crawled into the tent and zipped it shut. In the darkness, he stroked Willie's forehead. With his sleeping bag now zipped around him, David laid himself against Willie's right side, with his head touching Willie's cheek, so that if Willie stirred in the night he might wake up and try to get him to swallow. With the scent of Willie's hair and skin and clothes in his mind, and a glimmer of hope, David sank into the deep sleep of exhaustion.

David awakened in the dark. It seemed difficult to roll over. He lifted his head to watch Willie's breathing. Reassured, he lay down again. Something seemed strange. He lifted his head again and saw a sleeping bag on his other side. Lifting the top edge, he peered in the darkness at Alicia, sleeping soundly. David put his head down again and went to sleep.

## DESERT WILLOW

Bill Gluzack was tired and irritable. The tiny silver digits on the face of his wristwatch displayed five fifteen AM and here he was at the Backcountry Reservations Office. The telephone crews had just restored the lines into the Village, even though the snow continued. The storm ended during the night, as predicted. But now, a smaller, piggyback storm had taken its place.

He had come in at three this morning to wait for the Weather Service data to come on line. He and Jason Rantoon, a tall, pock-faced ranger in his mid twenties, had spent the last hour sifting through the information and making what phone calls they could. He was annoyed to learn that the line into the Canyon was likely to stay down for another day.

Gluzack was also irritated because Mandi Fisher had not climbed out yesterday. When he thought about it, he was not surprised that she had elected to wait for the storm to pass. Or maybe she would accompany the Hermit Loop party, due to climb out today. He remembered that Sanchez had planned to carry down some long instep crampons for them.

"When the weather breaks tomorrow," he said to Rantoon, "I want three of you to go down Bright Angel and sweep the area from the Silver Bridge to Hermit."

"If the weather breaks," the younger man added.

"It will," Gluzack insisted. "The weather man promised."

"But will I respect him in the morning?" Rantoon asked.


David opened his eyes. His head was touching Willie's right cheek. David's left arm was numb. I must have slept on it, he thought. All of his muscles ached with immobility. He felt as though he had not moved so much as his pinkie finger since he fell asleep last night. With a grunt, he lifted himself to his knees and prodded his flaccid arm. The sleeping bag sagged off his body. He saw that he was fully dressed. He also saw that Alicia was gone.

He looked at Willie's pale, relaxed face. He noticed that Willie still breathed in long slow sighs. The stuffed rabbit rested near his chin with his left arm draped over it. David absently scratched the rabbit's ears. He could not remember if he had placed the rabbit there the night before.

David's left arm began to hurt as the circulation returned. *Circulation!* How stupid to forget circulation, he scolded himself. The book had said to check the circulation of the leg to make sure the splint was not too tight. He had forgotten the circulation in Willie's left leg. He had left it in the splint for a day and a half without checking. He felt inept.

He took out his pocket knife and crawled over to Willie's left foot, which extended, along with the splint, beyond the sleeping bag, through the bottom of the two way zipper. Using the point of the blade, he carefully cut away the nylon upper from the toe of the boot. With more force, he carved at the suede rim. The knife slipped, pricking the side of Willie's big toe. He saw the toes move slightly beneath the socks. He pulled on the toe of Willie's wool sock, cut it open, then rolled back the sock. He repeated this with the liner sock. The toes looked awfully pale, he thought. But there was the drop of blood from the knife point. Satisfied, he unrolled the socks to cover the toes.

Next he checked the towel inside Willie's pants. It was still dry. With the sleeping bag pulled back, he studied Willie's smooth chest moving gently up and down. He placed his hand over Willie's heart, gaining hope from the warmth and rhythmic thump. He covered him and stroked his hair.

Exiting the tent, he closed the door behind him and went to his pack, which leaned against a desert willow. From it he took *Elements of Survival* and a zipper lock bag containing his toilet paper. The others were not up yet. He crossed the dry creek bed then headed up the hill toward the throne latrine, eighty yards away.


Jay Vesco lay in the misty region between sleep and wakefulness. He felt the warmth of Laura's head resting on his arm. This is truly good, he thought. He was pleased with himself when he recalled that he had made it with her twice last night. His only regret was her constantly bitching at him to slow down. None of the other girls had complained. But no matter how he looked at it, it was a truly awesome night.

He opened his eyes at the possibility that Mr. T might return and find her in his tent. That could get ugly. He put his clothes on quickly. Laura stirred, but remained asleep. Jay lifted the top of the sleeping bag and admired her bare breasts for a moment. This is the sight of a truly satisfied woman, he thought with pride. She probably doesn't realize how lucky she is. Jay had never before taken back a girl who had dumped him.

Jay unzipped the door of the tent with one rapid motion of his arm. There, twelve feet away, a ranger stood untying the one remaining sack of food.

"What are you doing?" Jay asked indignantly.

Surprised, the ranger spun his head around. Jay immediately recognized him as the strange, bearded man at Hermit Rapids.

"You cock sucker," yelled Jay as he surged forward to tackle the thief.

The man in the green ranger coat easily stepped aside to dodge the tackle. Jay scuffed the ground. When he turned to reach for him again, he stared into the barrel of a revolver.

"Shit, man," Jay said with a tremor in his voice and a sudden pounding in his chest, "take anything you want." He stood slowly and backed away with both hands extended to the sides. That the man now wore a ranger's coat, raised frightening questions in Jay's mind. He wondered if he would ever quarterback another football game.

Without altering the aim of the gun, the man shifted his eyes to Jay's tent. Laura had poked her head out. She raised her eyebrows and said nothing, apparently frozen by the sight of the gun. The man looked at the other two tents.

"Get everybody out of their tents," he said to Jay in a coarse voice.

"Sure." Jay walked to Laura's tent, the aim of the gun following him. "Hey, Alicia," he said in a loud voice, devoid of emotion, "you gotta get up."

The top corner of the door flap opened. Alicia's face looked up at Jay. "What is it?"

"You need to get dressed and come out right now."

"Is it Willie?" she asked, her voice suddenly infused with concern.

"No. But we have...kind of a problem."

"What?"

"Just do it," he demanded.

"Jay, what's going on?" she asked in exasperation.

"Well, there's this...ranger here.  He...wants to talk to everybody"

"Just a minute," she said.

Jay walked to Davie's tent. "Davie, get up." He unzipped the door and saw that Davie was gone.  He looked about the campsite, then scanned the horizon.  Looking back at the man, he shrugged and said, "He's not there."

"Wait over there," the man said to Laura, who had come out of the tent.  The man walked to Davie's tent.  Jay backed away.  He motioned to Jay with the gun, indicating that he should join Laura, and knelt to look into the tent.

"He's hurt really bad," Jay pointed out, in the way of an explanation for why he had not bothered to rouse Willie.

"Yeah," the man said, without taking his eyes off Willie.

Alicia gasped as she exited the tent and saw the gun.  She joined Jay and Laura without prompting.

"What do you want?" Laura asked.

The man did not answer, but looked over the equipment in the campsite.  "The tall, skinny kid, he's the one that's gone?"

"Yeah," answered Jay.

"Get some rope and tie the girls to the tree," he instructed Jay.

Jay found the rope and clumsily tied their hands behind their backs, then tied the two girls together around the waist, against the desert willow. *The fucker is going to kill us all.* He would wait for an opportunity to stop him.

"Dump out all the packs."

Jay did this.  He watched as the man selected Jay's own pack frame and dumped the contents of his stolen stuff sack into it.  He motioned Jay over to the tree.  Tucking his gun into his belt, he proceeded to tie Jay's hands.

Before his hands were joined, Jay wrenched them away and grabbed the man's coat lapels.  The man fluidly trapped Jays hands by placing his own on top, then squatted.  This dropped Jay to his knees.

Laura screamed, "No, don't hurt him."

"That was a really stupid thing to do," the man shouted. Plying Jay's little finger backwards in a finger lock, he turned him to the ground, drew his gun with the other hand and cocked the hammer. Jay squeezed his eyes shut. Laura screamed.

Jay wondered if he would hear the gun before he died, and if he would feel any pain. Five seconds passed. The pain eased on Jay's little finger. Jay opened his eyes. The man had not pulled the trigger. If he wanted to kill them all, Jay thought, he would have fired. Jay relaxed. The man released his finger. He was just going to steal what he wanted, Jay realized, then leave. Jay looked up as the man stood, his gun still cocked and aimed at Jay's face.

Jay breathed. He was going to live. He had not died cowering on the ground. And he was going to even things up if he ever got the chance.


David crouched behind blackbrush, observing the campsite twenty yards away. David knew now that this man was the escaped killer from the radio news. Seeing him there, beside Jay, David felt that Jay was the more dangerous of the two. He had no doubt that Jay would have pulled the trigger without hesitation.

The man instructed Jay to lie face down, then tied his hands and feet together behind him. David watched the man rifle through the pile of belongings, tossing some into one of the backpacks. It puzzled David, and annoyed him to see the thief remove the lashing straps from David's pack, and throw them into the commandeered pack. He took rope, and the remaining food and fuel. He seemed satisfied to find the topographic map of the Canyon. After throwing in several more water bottles, he closed the pack. The man walked over to David's tent and touched Willie's forehead. David felt a brief surge of indignation. *Don't touch him!* But David kept his silence. The man in the ranger coat hefted the pack and headed east on the Tonto. David watched him climb out of Horn Creek drainage, waited another two minutes, just to make sure, then went down into the campsite.

"Oh, God," Laura said, "that guy was here!"

"I know." David nodded as he walked to the tree where the girls were tied. "I watched him from up there."

"And you didn't help?" Jay growled.

"I'm helping now," David replied, untying Laura and Alicia.

"You're such a worthless faggot," Jay continued. "How about untying me? Or is that too much to ask?"

"Knock it off, Jay," Laura said in David's defense. She touched David's shoulder. "Thanks."

"So, now you're sticking up for that chicken shit queer?" Jay said, rolling his eyes.

Laura stared at Jay for a moment. "Sometimes, you make me sick," she mumbled.

David met Alicia's gaze. He caught a fleeting smile. He did feel worthless and helpless. The man could have shot all three of them and he would only have been able to watch. And he certainly didn't understand Alicia. He went into his tent and zipped it shut.

He sat and watched Willie's breathing. Then the tears came to him. He held Willie's hand to his cheek and cried.

Willie's smaller hand weakly grasped David's hand. David sat up straight, looking at the hand. Willie's face frowned in agony. Willie groaned softly.

"Oh God, Willie," he whispered, leaning over to Willie's ear, "It's okay. You're going to be alright. We're going to get you help."

Willie cracked his eyelids, then weakly squeezed David's hand again.

"Willie, you have to drink something. I know it's hard," he whispered at his ear, "but I'll help you."

He lifted Willie's head and gave him tiny sips of water, which he swallowed.

"That's good, Willie." David continued to feel tears flowing over his cheeks. He opened his jacket pocket and took out a little packet of acetaminophen, which he opened with his teeth.

"This is a pill, Willie. Do you think you can swallow it?" Willie did not answer. "You've got to take it." David separated Willie's lips and placed it at the tip of his tongue. After a little more water, the pill was gone. He gave him another, followed by more water.

"Davie?"  It was Alicia's voice outside the tent.

"Just unzip the door, Alicia," he said.

She unzipped it and looked at David, surprised to see him with one arm under Willie's head, the other holding a water bottle.

"He woke up a little."

Alicia touched Willie's forehead with her fingers.  The gesture carried such a burden of tenderness that David's tears returned. His eyes met Alicia's, but he felt no shame in his tears.

She placed her hand on David's knee. "What should we do, Davie?", her words soaked in despair.  "I think something must have happened to Mr. Thurman."

"I don't know," David admitted.

Alicia gently wiped the tears from David's face.

"We've got to hide somewhere," Jay said from nearby, "in case that guy comes back."

Alicia's eyes pleaded with David to offer some alternative to Jay's opinion.

"Well," David said, as he groped for some wisdom, "Willie needs help, but we'd have to take him the same way the man went.  We need to wait for help to come to us, but I don't think we should stay here."

"So what should we do?" she asked again.

Laura knelt in front of the tent.  "We need your ideas, Davie," Laura said, stroking her brother's hair.

"Look," Jay said, "I found a great place to hide in the back of this canyon.  I say we go there and wait for somebody to come."

David laid Willie's head down.  "How far is it, Jay?"

"I don't know, maybe a mile.  But we need to get the fuck out of here now, in case that killer comes back."

"Can you walk that far?" David asked, looking at Alicia.

"I think so."

"Then we need to get our stuff together and pack the tents," David concluded.

"You don't need a tent," Jay insisted. "This is a cave we're going to."

David looked at Laura.  She nodded.

SSgt. Jeffrey Horn approached the Tapeats cliff where Thurman had fallen. He looked over the edge at the body far below. Envy, was what he felt. Envy. But his courage was gone. He walked farther, then detoured to look again at the ranger he had shot. On the outcrop of rock, fifteen feet below, he saw nothing except a pair of binoculars with one tube caved in. The ranger was gone. There was no blood. He looked farther down. Then he saw a route, just below his feet, which could have allowed her to climb from the outcrop.

He spun about and studied the horizon. She was alive, somewhere, and still had her gun. She must have headed back to Indian Garden. Or maybe not.

Horn crossed the trail and found a secluded spot between two boulders. There he opened the map and studied possible routes of escape, and places to hide.

## MOTHER CAVE

David struggled alongside Laura at the rear of the makeshift stretcher. Jay held the front end, as they carried Willie toward Jay's hiding place. Alicia hobbled behind, her ankle injury too painful to allow her to assist. David noticed that it appeared less swollen this morning.

Thirty minutes after setting out from Horn Creek Campsite, they reached the ridge of the intervening shale slope. David remembered how flat the Tonto platform had appeared from the Rim. Standing on the gray-green fragments of Bright Angel shale, David could read the reality of its steep slopes and boulder-strewn ravines in the pain and fatigue of his muscles. The fatigue was made less tolerable by his uncertainty about how long this ordeal would continue.

David looked up to the caves near the top of the Redwall. Those would be a wonderful place to hide, he thought, a place to be free of the gnawing fear that had possessed him since he watched the man point his gun at Jay's face. He looked at the two caves lower in the Redwall. The lowest seemed about thirty feet above the crumbled scree slope. His heart pounded. No other caves were visible.

"Hold up a minute," he said to Jay. They lowered the stretcher to the sloped shale.

"What?" Jay asked, only a little less winded than David.

"Where exactly is this cave?" David asked, hoping he did not know the answer already.

"Right there," Jay answered proudly. He pointed toward the cave David had feared was the one.

Laura looked at Jay with disgust, then turned to David expectantly.

"Let's just get everybody to those boulders," David said with quiet resignation. "We can go back for the rest of the gear then." David indicated the fallen, house-size chunks of Redwall resting in the ravine near the head of the side-canyon.

"I never said it was easy, asshole," Jay interjected in his own defense.

David looked at Willie, on the stretcher, and at Alicia limping to catch up. To reach the cave, they would have to scramble up ninety feet of sliding scree, which sloped at a frightening sixty degrees, then climb thirty vertical feet of cliff. David knew words were useless. They continued with Willie, passing the lowest cave, one hundred twenty feet above them, and reached the boulders by ascending the ravine at the head of Horn Creek's western branch.

David found a relatively flat and stable area with a partial view of the side canyon. There they placed Willie.

"It doesn't seem like the cave is much of an advantage," David began, "since two of us can't get up there, and...I don't want to climb a cliff."

"We already know you're chicken shit," Jay responded, "but I don't see any reason why I have to just sit here and wait to get shot."

Laura looked at David. She said nothing, apparently waiting for a better suggestion, waiting for David to decide. *Why me?* David stared at his size fifteen boots while he gathered his thoughts.

"At first aid shelters, fire signals of wet food," David said, remembering the passage from Elements of Survival that he had reread that morning at the latrine. "It's the priorities for survival in the wilderness."

They stared blankly at him.

"It's a mnemonic for remembering the priorities: attitude, first aid, shelter, fire, signal, water, food. The most important is attitude. We have to think about what we need to do, and know that we'll make it out okay."

"Fuck attitude," shouted Jay, "I'm going up to the cave. You can stay here with Davie to protect you," he said to Laura, "or you can come up to the cave, where that maniac with the gun can never get to you."

"What about my brother and Alicia?" Laura asked coldly.

"Not my problem. You guys can...I don't know. Fuck it, I'm going up." Jay turned and headed up the scree.

Laura watched Jay begin to work his way toward the cave. She sighed and turned back to David. "Tell me about those priorities, Davie," Laura said.

"I think I want to hear too, Davie," added Alicia.

David recalled the lectures on less important matters that his father had aimed at him over the years. "After attitude is first aid. I think we've done all we can. Then shelter, in case it's cold or wet. Later, we can go back and get a couple of tents. Fire is for warmth or morale or for a signal. I don't think we need one for any of those. We could make a signal, but it would have to be visible only from the air, so that crazy guy can't see it."

"Maybe we could have like a flag or something, that we could wave if somebody else came by," Alicia suggested.

"That's good. And we can make a big X across the ground, in case an airplane flies by. Shelter...fire... signal...water. We definitely need more water."

"We can get it down stream from the campsite," Laura suggested.

"That might be the first place that guy would go to, if he needed water. We could try this branch of the creek."

"That's a better idea," Laura agreed.

"And the very last priority is food," David concluded.

"I'm not hungry, anyway," Alicia said.

"You will be," he warned.

"Davie," Laura said with excitement, "Willie's moving."

They crowded around Willie, who grimaced and lifted his right arm. He opened his frowning eyes and reached toward David, who took his hand. Willie pulled his hand away from David and touched his own crotch.

David thought for a moment, then leaned close to Willie's ear and whispered, "It's okay to pee, if you need to. I stuffed a towel in your pants."

Willie squeezed David's arm and relaxed, though the pain never left his face.

"Drink some water, Willie," David said.

Willie turned his head slightly away.

"You have to drink, Willie." David opened the one water bottle that was not empty, and offered some to Willie, lifting his head.

"I'll go find some more water," Laura offered.

"You shouldn't go alone," David said.    "How about if Alicia stays here to help Willie, and the two of us go for water?"

"That's fine with me," Alicia agreed.

David took Alicia aside. He was embarrassed. "Did you ever change your little brother's diapers?"

"Yeah, why?

"Well...never mind." David wasn't sure if he was more embarrassed for Willie or himself. "Never mind."

David took the three remaining water bottles and tied them with the remaining nylon rope, to make a sling for carrying over his shoulder. Laura took only her walking stick. The two of them headed down the drainage of the western branch of Horn Creek. As they descended, they looked up occasionally to watch Jay's progress in his senseless climb to the cave.


Jay scrambled up the scree, slipping down with each step almost as much as he climbed. He couldn't believe how stupid Laura was acting. He saw a diagonal ridge forty yards to his left. He thought it reached up to a ledge at the base of the cliff. Ten minutes of fierce scrambling brought him to the diagonal ridge. Once there, he found that he could rapidly climb the scree along this crack in the slope.

At the top, the ledge stretched to his right. It was wide enough for side stepping, he thought, but too narrow to allow him to walk. Jay made his way along the ledge. About half way to the point below the cave, the erosion of the ledge required him to use his hands on the rock above to prevent his feet from slipping off. He held his breath for the ten foot section of erosion, then breathed again as he resumed the side step to the point immediately beneath the cave. He saw thirty feet of vertical cliff separating him from the cave entrance.

Using his fingertips and the toes of his boots, Jay moved upward. His heart pounding, he closed his eyes. There he saw the vision that had haunted him since Willie's fall: the purple, nylon jacket extending its arms and sailing, tumbling in the air.

Both of Jay's feet slipped from the ledge. Hanging by his fingers on the shallow ledge, he groped with his feet until they found purchase. He opened his eyes to drive away the vision.

Continuing upward, he reached the dust coated slope of

the cave entrance. He plopped his torso onto the slope and scrambled to keep from sliding back out. The floor of the cave felt warm and safe.


David could see that he and Laura would have difficulty following the dry creek bed to water. The descent was impeded by numerous small cliffs and narrow passages.

"Look what I found, Davie."

David turned and saw Laura studying an antler dropped by a mule deer.

"Give me some of your rope," she said.

"I don't have much left," David replied, unsure if they could afford to waste any of it.

"Give me about half of that," she clarified, nodding toward the white nylon rope David had used to create a comfortable sling for carrying the water bottles across his shoulders.

David handed her all the rope, with the three empty water bottles attached. He found a flat rock and sat down. Laura accepted the rope and sat beside him to untangle it.

"You got a knife?" she asked.

David extracted a small jackknife from a zippered pants pocket. With the rope, Laura lashed her newly discovered deer antler to the top of her walking stick. David watched silently as she worked the rope with surprising skill, probably the result, he guessed, of having to frequently retie the lashings on Willie's pack frame stretcher. She cut off three feet of rope, which she returned to David, then completed the lash, trimming away a three inch piece of rope that extended beyond her lashing. As David strung the lid loops of the water bottles together, he studied Laura's new construction.

"It's a weapon," she said simply. "Let's go."

"I think we should follow the base of the Tapeats to the river," David suggested. "A weapon?"

"It makes me feel better. Do we really have to go to the river?"

"This is just getting harder here. I read about a way to reach the river by following the bottom of the Tapeats."

"I'm easy," Laura replied. "Lead on."

Jay looked up to the shadowy crack through the length of the cave roof. It sloped downward toward the rear. As his eyes adjusted to the darkness, he noticed a military ammo box on the cave floor, ten feet away.

His first thought was that it was a trap, a bomb or something. With growing curiosity, he approached the box and opened the latch, half expecting a nasty surprise. He lifted the lid. Inside were a spiral notebook and a pencil. Jay read the notebook's label, "MOTHER CAVE REGISTRY." Mother cave, he thought. *Cool.* The notebook contained a list of names with dates. An entry dated a year ago bore the name, Maria Sanchez, whom he recognized as the ranger at the BRO. Further down the page were the names of five Boy Scouts, complete with their troop number and ages—thirteen and fourteen years old. Jay found those entries comforting. *If a bunch of faggot Scouts can climb up here and get back down....* He proudly signed his name and the date, then returned the registry to the ammo box and latched it.

Jeffrey Horn walked west again on the Tonto. He had identified a spot on the topographic map that was off the trail and would allow him access to water, as well as a place to hide. He recognized that he had made several potentially fatal mistakes since entering the Canyon, but somehow had been lucky enough to survive them.

As he walked in the late morning gray, he recalled one of his lectures at Fairchild. As an instructor, his task is to teach the survival students how to behave in captivity. They must put aside pride and bravado to survive, while in the hands of the enemy.

> *"While you are a prisoner," Horn says to the class, "your words and actions will determine whether or not you survive. Sometimes you will be punished for your actions or insults without understanding what you have done to offend your captors.*
> *"One Viet Nam POW tells of his interrogation after being shot down. He was taken into a room and seated on a chair. He answered a few simple questions*

*to the satisfaction of his interrogator. Then, without warning, he was slapped across the face so hard that it knocked him off the chair. He was returned to his cell. This sequence of events was repeated for three days without explanation. On the fourth day he recognized that the unprovoked slap occurred when he crossed his legs. He later learned that showing the bottom of your foot is considered an insult, something like giving the finger.*

*"More to the point of your training experience here, you may be tempted to play John Wayne or Rambo when confronted with a difficult situation. It is that attitude that will get you tortured or killed. Now, since killing our students doesn't help them to improve their skills, we will, instead, use a code word. That word is 'stress'. If you hear the word, stress, during your resistance training, it means that you just screwed up. It means that, in the hands of the enemy, you would probably be killed for it. Or worse."*

That lecture was only fifteen months ago.

Horn descended the trail toward the campsite where he had encountered the teenagers this morning. He knew the tall skinny one, the missing one, would have untied the others by now, and they all would have fled.

He recognized that he had almost shot the other, athletic boy, even though he had not chosen to shoot him. He would have said, "Do you understand the meaning of the word 'stress'?"

But, instead, his finger had tightened on the trigger. It was close. A different gun, he thought, would have fired. *It was close.*

Horn looked through the belongings left behind. In the zippered side pocket of one of the backpacks he found a pack of cigarettes, only a few missing. He sat down against the desert willow to which the kids had been tied and lit a cigarette.

He knew that his life was over. They would do everything possible to capture him here. And if somehow they failed, then they would pick apart the entire country until they found him.

He looked again at the spot where he had almost shot the boy earlier. There is such a fragile boundary between being alive and being dead forever. It was an easy one to cross. Had he squeezed the trigger one fraction more, the boy would be dead now. But the difference between dying and killing himself seemed a more durable barrier. It had dissolved briefly yesterday, he recalled. Today it was insurmountable. He would have to be killed by some power that he did not control: the ranger with the gun, the marshals, or perhaps the Canyon itself. But it would not come by his own hand. And if his instinct for survival came into play, he knew he would resist.

SSgt. Jeffrey Horn extinguished the cigarette, field stripped it, and sprinkled the remaining tobacco into the rocks with a toss of his arm. He placed the filter and paper into his jacket pocket and headed west on the Tonto Trail.


David followed a narrow trace northward along the seam between the Tapeats and the Vishnu, until they reached the final pitch that dropped to the river. It was a steep but solid slope of black Vishnu schist ending abruptly at Horn Creek rapids. Using their hands against the smooth rock for balance, they made their way down the eight hundred foot slope to the edge of the surging brown water.

David filled the three water bottles and added two purification tablets to each, since the water appeared muddy, once it was in the bottle.

"Let's wait here for twenty minutes," David suggested, "drink as much as we can, then refill the bottles."

"I think I need to rest twenty minutes before I can climb back up that slope, anyway," Laura replied. Laura had seemed quieter than usual all day. Her gaze was distant and her mood dark. They sat together on the slope.

"I'm glad you're here, Davie."

David looked at her with a sadness born of so many abrupt disturbances to his world. He felt awkward. Knew he was awkward. He also remembered the years of ridicule that he had endured from Laura. He remembered times when she had gone out of her way to make him feel inadequate and unattractive. Her casual humiliations of Willie had often included him as well. He had no doubt that if Jay were here, she would not bother talking with him.

"I think you saved Willie's life," she continued.

"I don't know that he's going to live. I didn't tell anybody, but he peed bright red blood the day it happened. And now he's dehydrated."

"But you've stayed with him every minute. He's lucky to have a friend like you."

David felt even more awkward. He was reminded that he hadn't really liked Willie all that much. But events had changed that. "I feel selfish, in a way, because I'm afraid that he'll die."

"But that's a good kind of selfish, to need somebody that you care about."

David wasn't sure. *Need?* He wondered what she was suggesting. This whole Canyon ordeal was tearing peep holes in the comfortable curtain of his solitary, educated existence. He was an only child and was quite content with the solitude and independence that represented.

"Davie, I don't understand how he fell. He's always been afraid to get near anything he could fall off of. When we were eleven, he wouldn't even climb up on the garage roof with me. And that's only twelve feet off the ground. I think the only way he made it down Hermit gorge was because he couldn't see it in the dark."

David decided not to discuss his suspicions about Jay's role in the accident. If Willie lived and implicated Jay, so be it. But David wasn't about to butt heads with someone so unpredictable, at least not now.

"I wish none of this had ever happened," he said.

"I'm really worried about my dad." Laura's eyes filled with tears. She tried to say more, but could not.

David took her hand. It felt like Willie's hand, only stronger.

"Do you think my father is alive?" she asked.

David didn't think so. "I don't know. Maybe he's hurt and can't get back to us."

Laura held his head between her hands and looked directly into his eyes. "You think he's dead, don't you, Davie?"

David hesitated. Through his tear filled eyes, David read the fear and unspeakable loss in a face that so closely resembled Willie's face. He hugged her. "Yes."

They cried together, then drank their fill of water. After refilling the bottles in the river and adding more tablets, they headed up the black Vishnu.

Jeffrey Horn veered from the Tonto trail and descended a dry creek bed. He could no longer consider any plan that required him to go to his pursuers. They would have to come and find him, at least until he could think it all through a little more clearly. It was a nightmare that would not end. He removed the stolen pack and the green coat, sat down on a flat rock and lit a cigarette. On the ground between his boots he saw a three inch piece of eighth-inch white nylon rope. The freshly cut end was bright white. Taking a long drag on the cigarette, he closed his eyes.

*He is in the Cascade Mountains. The air is crisp, moist. His black uniform labels him as a "goon," the enemy. He comes upon two careless students sitting in a small clearing in the forest. One student faces away from him, the other is occupied with untying his boot. They wear mud-encrusted flight suits.*

*"On the ground, American Pigs!" he shouts. Horn brandishes an empty AK-47.*

*They both look up in shock, their faces amateurishly decorated with camo makeup. The boot tying student, taller than the other, ignores Horn's command and returns to his boot. Horn places the butt of his gun onto the student's chest and shoves him backwards, toppling him over.*

*"Hey, man," the taller student says, "what's your problem?"*

*"Cool it, Jaws," his partner advises, with a scarcely hidden smile across his camo face.*

*"No, I'm not gonna cool it. This is just a God damn game."*

*"Stand up. Now!" Horn orders.*

*They both stand up with leisurely amusement.*

*Horn feels anger and frustration. This, he reminds himself, is just the kind of smartass bravado that got too many American flight crews killed during the war. Horn walks around them twice, trying to think of a way to get the message across. He sees that the taller student wears a huge Schrade hunting knife. Horn unsnaps the keeper and draws the student's blade to examine it. The edge appears to have been painstakingly honed and stropped.*

*"Just put it back, mother fucker," the tall student warns.*

*Horn looks into his eyes and sees more than anger. With a casual flick of the blade, Horn cuts the white, eighth-inch parachute cord that holds together the student's improvised pack strap. The pack falls to the ground.*

*"That was a really limp-dick thing to do," the student hisses.*

*Horn tosses the knife on the ground behind him. "Lieutenant," he says with an even voice, "do you understand the term 'stress'?"*

*"Do you understand the term limp-dick?" the student retorts.*

*Horn turns away, and stares briefly at the canopy of trees. He just doesn't get it. Still facing away he says, "I'm afraid I have to report to the Commander that you have just failed this course. You will have to make arrangements with your squadron to return at..."*

*Horn's words are interrupted by the sharp pain of a punch to his right kidney. Instinctively, he spins around, thrusting the butt of his AK-47 toward the student's chest. The student deflects the gun butt, it veers upward, striking full force into the student's throat. The sound of crushing cartilage is unmistakable and sickening. The tall student falls to the ground, choking and coughing blood.*

*His partner turns his camo covered face to Horn and shouts, "What's the matter with you? It's just a game!"*

*Horn steps over to the choking student and sees that he is dying. He will have to attempt emergency surgery to open the airway. A simple puncture of the tough membrane just below the larynx. He has never tried it before, but he knows he can do it. He reaches for the slender sheath knife at his belt.*

*Before he draws it, he sees the shorter student lunging at him with uncontrolled rage, the huge Schrade knife in his right hand. In a single sweeping movement, Horn deflects the knife with his right hand, grappling the knife arm. The student's body spins in the same direction. Horn crushes the pressure points of the student's wrist, drives the knuckles of his left fist behind the right ear, and sweeps his left boot edge into the student's left knee, striking the pressure points along its inner surface. The student collapses to the ground in a daze.*

*Horn kneels over the tall student and draws his own knife. The larynx is crushed. He can not tell where to make a cut. Tentatively, he presses the point of the blade into the student's neck. Dark blood wells up. Horn is smitten by his helplessness. He sheaths his knife and runs into the forest.*

Horn's thoughts returned to the Canyon, the wind echoing up from the inner gorge. He opened his eyes. He felt disoriented. The cigarette had burned down to the filter and gone out. He put the filter into a pocket and stood by his pack. The green coat lay beside it. He remembered that it came out of death. He wished someone could take him away from all this. He drew the gun from his belt and wondered why he had kept it. It had only made things worse. He set the gun onto the green coat.

When Jeffrey Horn turned around, he found the tall skinny boy and the white girl, four feet away. Time dilated. He could not understand why they were moving toward him. They should be running away. There was fear in the boy's eyes, but hatred in the girl's. She lunged at him.

*Deflect the stick. It's not right. An antler.*

He saw it tied to the stick, and plunged toward his right chest.

*No time.*

Pain wracked his body. He looked up to see the two kids running up the trail.

Horn looked down at the antler and the stick, still protruding from his chest, just below his right nipple. He was short of breath. Each breath hurt as much as the original thrust of the antler. With both hands, he pulled it out.

A sucking chest wound. He had heard the term, but had never heard the hideous sound of it until now. He tore open his shirt and saw a one inch slit that hissed with each breath and bubbled tiny amounts of blood.  The pain was scarcely bearable. *I may die here.  I might not die for a long time.  Oh, God.*

## REDWALL

David's legs carried him faster and farther with each step than ever before in his life.  Fleeing from a killer was definitely a factor, but five days in the Canyon had hardened his body.  His legs ached with fatigue, and yet they bounded him upward.  He heard Laura close behind.  Without a backpack, the cliffs and boulders seemed smaller, less daunting.

He had exchanged no words with Laura since their sudden encounter with the man.  David knew that they must return to the others and break for Indian Garden while the man was west of them.  If he caught them now, he might kill them all.

David passed beneath the entrance to Jay's cave.  He was afraid to yell, afraid of possibly alerting the man they had run from at the base of the Tapeats.  He continued up the drainage, knowing that his legs would last long enough to reach the boulders that hid Willie and Alicia.  Laura stayed with him, also passing the cave silently.

As he approached the boulders, David could make out Alicia's eyes peeking above the rock.  She stood as they neared.  She seemed concerned.

"What's the matter?" Alicia asked.

David was out of breath.  "We ran into that man, part way down the creek."

"Oh, God, Alicia, I stuck him with a deer antler, and it just stuck there," Laura said, the words tumbling out.  "We came around a corner in the trail and he was just standing there, staring."

"Laura found this deer antler and lashed it to her walking stick," David explained, "and when we saw him, she stuck him in the chest."

"So what happened?" Alicia asked.

"It just stuck there," Laura continued, "and wouldn't come out. Oh, it felt so horrible. I just left it there and ran."

"Did he follow you?" Alicia looked down the drainage. David followed her gaze.

"I never saw him after that." Against the eastern slope of the drainage, he saw a faint, twenty foot 'X' traced into the rocks.

"Did you do that, Alicia?" he asked, pointing toward it.

"There wasn't much to use," she answered, "so I lined up the rocks. I don't think you can see it except from above."

"That's nice, Alicia," he said, knowing that the weather on the Rim would keep the planes grounded.

"And I made this." Alicia held up her walking stick with Willie's purple, nylon jacket tied on by the sleeves.

"Have you seen Jay since he climbed up to the cave?" Laura asked.

"Not since he got up there."

David knelt by Willie, who appeared to sleep. He absently scratched the ears of his rabbit, Ezra. Willie kept it clutched against his neck.

Alicia leaned down to David. "He peed."

David looked at her uncomfortably.

"I dried the towel for a while, then put it back."

David smiled sheepishly and nodded. Placing the towel had seemed such a personal and private act for David. Alicia could probably never understand that. But Alicia continued to mystify him. She was unquestionably a kind and loving person, but the object of her love still escaped David's understanding. He stood and looked up at the massive Redwall, which dominated the side-canyon.

"I think we should head for Indian Garden," David said, "before that guy beats us to it." David looked up at the cave.

"Jay," Laura yelled. "Jay."

David saw nothing moving at the cave entrance. When Laura looked at him, he could only shrug his shoulders. Laura was no less a mystery than Alicia. The hidden strands of allegiance between Laura and Jay, Laura and Willie, and even Laura and David himself, gave David a sensation of smothering. Maybe this would set his father straight concerning the improbability of, "You'll understand when you're older." David comforted himself with the assurance that, when he was older, he would still not be able to figure out this morass of emotions and loyalties.

"I'll climb up," Laura volunteered.

David touched her shoulder. "It looks dangerous."

"So's getting shot," she said flatly.

"It'll take a long time," Alicia added. "It took Jay almost a half hour to get up there...and he slipped twice. It was scary to watch."

"That's an hour, round trip," David pointed out, "if you make it without breaking your neck."

"Jay," Laura yelled again. "I've never seen him like this."

Then you haven't been looking very hard, David thought in response. How could she find something to like about that selfish, cruel, insensitive asshole?

They all sat down. David handed a water bottle to Alicia. "It's already treated."

Alicia opened it and drank.

"How's your leg?" David asked.

"It's definitely better," Alicia said between gulps, "but it's still painful to walk."

"Do you think we can carry Willie without Jay?" he asked.

"We'll have to," Laura said without conviction.

"Somebody's coming," Alicia whispered, peering over the rock.

David looked. The green ranger's coat was unmistakable. The man in the ranger coat walked with his head lowered, clutching the right side of his chest, a gun in the other hand. David's breathing accelerated. He heard the pounding of blood within his ears. Laura clutched his left arm painfully. This was it, he realized. All those meaningless concerns about who loves who, who touched who, all his agony over Willie, everything was over. They were all going to die now. All except Jay.

"It's somebody different," Alicia whispered. "The man this morning was bald on top."

*What is she saying?* David looked with new eyes. This was a woman.

"It's a ranger," David said, tears filling his eyes. "It's a ranger." He slumped down against the rock and closed his eyes.

Alicia stood above the rock and waved Willie's purple jacket. "Up here! We're up here!" she shouted.

David stood up; his legs barely complied. The uphill sprint had drained him. He vaguely recognized the ranger as the woman from the BRO.

"You guys look kind of beat up," the ranger said.

"Am I glad to see you," Laura blurted out, hugging the ranger.

"I was pretty worried when I saw the tents and stuff down there abandoned," the ranger continued. "Tell me what's happened, Laura."

"Yesterday," David said, "Willie fell.... No two days ago Willie fell off a dry waterfall at Salt Creek. He broke his leg and was unconscious until this morning."

"Let's see," the ranger said. She walked over to Willie. I'm Maria," she said to David. "You're..?"

"David, and this is Alicia."

"Where's your other friend?"

"Jay?" Laura asked. "He climbed up there this morning," she pointed to the cave, "and hasn't answered when we call him."

Maria knelt by Willie and examined him, while David and Laura related their two encounters with the man.

"I know the waterfall at Salt Creek. It's hard to believe he survived. Willie," Maria called, "Willie."

"He wakes up every few hours," David said. "He's in a lot of pain then."

"I'll bet," she said, gently caressing his cheek. David watched with apprehension as Maria lifted both eyelids with her thumbs, then began at the top and felt his head and face, never lifting or turning it. She unzipped the sleeping bag and pressed her ear to each side of his bare chest. Her fingers traced the course of each rib. Maria listened to his abdomen, then pressed it in several places. With a hand on either side of his hips, she pressed toward the center. She looked under his pants, lifting the towel.

"He's been urinating?"

David explained about the blood and its subsequent clearing. He told about the water he had been forcing Willie to drink.

While Maria felt Willie's right leg, Laura explained about the wounds on his back and left buttock. David was most uncomfortable when the ranger inspected the traction splint and the cut boot, exposing Willie's toes. She tightened the traction a little, then stood.

"Who made this splint?" she asked.

"I did," David said with hesitation. "I tried to do it exactly like the book explained it."

Maria put her arm around David, then included Alicia and Laura. "You guys are really something." She smiled the broadest smile David had seen in days. "I saw your father with Sergeant Horn," she said to Laura, "but I don't know what's happened to him, because Horn shot me. No, it's okay. I was really lucky. I had binoculars around my neck and son-of-a-gun if the bullet didn't hit the binoculars. It just left a big bruise. But I fell over a ledge and was out for a while. When I woke up, they were both gone."

"He would have come back, if he could," Laura said flatly.

Maria squeezed the back of Laura's neck. "We're not out of this yet. We need to get to Indian Garden today. If the phone lines are still out, then we have to climb out in the morning with Willie on a stretcher." She looked at Laura. "Call your friend one more time. If he won't climb down, then we'll have to come get him later."

Alicia and Laura walked toward the cave.

The ranger put both of her hands on David's shoulders. "That's the best damn traction splint I've ever seen in the field. But before I award you an M.D., we need to brace his head, in case he has a neck injury."

"I hope he doesn't, because I've been lifting his head to help him drink." David shuddered at the thought of Willie paralyzed from the neck down.

"Then he probably doesn't, but we should brace his head just to be safe."

David watched silently as Maria took Willie's purple jacket from the pole. Holding its arms outstretched, she folded its body over to make one long piece of fabric, which she laid across his forehead and tied to the siderails of the stretcher.

"This will have to do for now," she said.

"Do you think he's going to make it, Maria?"

She looked in his eyes, a sad smile on her lips. "He might, David. He just might. But you've done a heck of a job of keeping him alive. Some other time, you'll have to tell me how you learned all this."

Jay did not answer when Laura called up to the cave again.

"Let's go," Maria called. "We'll have to send someone for him later."

With Maria carrying the front of the stretcher, David and Laura carrying the rear, they hiked across the shale slopes. Alicia walked behind. They descended to the campsite, then continued east along the Tonto.

Where the Tonto Trail skirts the edge of the Tapeats, they stopped. David stood near the cliff, trying in his mind to separate the beauty from the horror. Terraces and temples, stacked one upon another, stretched their subdued palette to the horizon, beneath the unending gray of Arizona winter. It had seemed so beautiful only a few days ago. He looked at the pie crust of the Tapeats across the river, realizing that he stood at the edge of an equally precipitous cliff. Beneath him, the earth appeared to fall away. A hundred feet below, the horror returned. David saw the contorted body of Mr. Thurman. He backed away, bumping into Maria. She looked at him intensely and nodded her head almost imperceptibly. David realized that he wasn't really surprised to find Mr. Thurman dead. It seemed to follow the twisted plot of the entire trek.

"Let's go," Maria said.

He took up the corner of Willie's stretcher and continued along the trail to Indian Garden. At the intersection with the wider tourist trail, David could finally walk on the trail itself, instead of its shoulders. With a sweet feeling of accomplishment, David entered the canopy of yellow cottonwoods and reached the ranger station.

"Lets get Willie onto a real stretcher. The three of you will have to lift him while I control his head."

They moved Willie to an aluminum frame evacuation basket, and anchored his head with a wide Velcro strap. David stayed by Willie, watching Maria as she did for Willie what he had only dreamed of doing for two days. With amazing speed and skill, Maria started an intravenous line in Willie's right arm and hung a liter bag of IV fluid.

"I'm going to run in half of this bag wide open, to see if we can get some urine. David, let me know when the bag's half empty."

"He doesn't have to swallow it, either," David observed.

"The phone is still out, but my boss will send help down in the morning just because you guys didn't climb out today. If the line is still out in the morning, we'll carry Willie on this litter and hope some fresh muscle power arrives before too long."
Maria mixed a small bottle of medicine and injected it into the IV tubing.

"What are you giving him?" David asked.

"A big hit of antibiotics for the mess on his back."

"I didn't think park rangers would know that kind of stuff."

"Well, everybody gets first aid training, but I worked as a paramedic in San Antonio before I joined the Park Service. So when I tell you that's a good pack frame stretcher, it's no bullshit."

Willie was going to live, David thought. He's really going to live. For the first time in days, David sensed a cause for genuine optimism.

"You watch the bag, doctor David. Laura, would you come in the back for a minute."

David watched them go, then called Alicia over. "We saw Mr. Thurman's body at the bottom of a cliff today. I think Maria's telling Laura about it now."

"I think Laura already knew," Alicia replied, showing very little emotion. "I think everybody sort of knew."

When Laura returned, David saw no tears, but he had the impression that Laura's shoulders sagged more than they had when she went in. Laura looked at him briefly, then knelt by her brother. She kissed Willie's forehead above the Velcro strap. David watched dumbly as she struggled to control her emotions. She folded her face to her knees and cried. David looked up at Alicia. His gaze seemed to cause Alicia to cry. He looked away, choked by the pain.

"Let's go outside," Alicia whispered to Laura.

David listened to their footsteps and heard the door close. David was now alone again with Willie. Willie's color looked better since the IV was running. David held his hand.

"Put these under the towel to soak up the urine," Maria said, holding out four bulky sanitary napkins, "with this side up."

"I think the bag's about half gone," David pointed out.

"Close enough for government work." She slowed the IV. She smiled and disappeared into the back.

David placed the sanitary napkins beneath the towel in Willie's pants.  For a while, he watched the clear solution dripping in the chamber of the IV tubing.  He looked at the toes on Willie's left foot.  They were pink.

He thought of Jay pushing Willie off the waterfall.  Jay had nearly caused Alicia to drown.  The worst part of it was that Jay didn't recognize anything wrong with the things he did.  And the cave.  He had led them all to a place where only he was safe.  How had Mr. Thurman admired someone like that?  Somehow Mr. Thurman had died without Jay's help.  If Jay never came down from the cave, David decided, that would be just fine.

David shared a supper of assorted snack bars, left at the ranger station by dozens of hikers.  Maria told him that it was not unusual for backpackers to discover, after their first day of canyon hiking, that their grocery shopping had been overzealous.

His exhaustion now seemed to supersede his hunger.  David and each of the others found their separate corners for the night.

As David sat beside Willie, he realized that, for the first time in days, he could allow himself to fall asleep without the specter of awakening to find Willie dead.  His thoughts were interrupted by the soft sound of footsteps.

"Mind if I sit here for a while?" Alicia whispered.

"Pull up a chair," David whispered back, indicating an adjacent patch of wood floor.

"He looks better," she said, brushing the hair from Willie's forehead.

"I think he's going to be okay."

"Davie..." Alicia paused, nervously pressing a crease into her jeans with her fingers.  "Does Willie have a girlfriend?  I mean, I never really see him, like dating."

David shifted uncomfortably.  He wasn't sure what she might be getting at.  "What do you mean?"

"Well, like...I always see him with you, but not with any girls."

"You're starting to sound like Jay."  She was half the problem, he thought.  She's the one who disappeared from the tent.

"No, that's not what I mean."

"He's hurt.  I thought he was going to die.  Nobody else stayed by him."

"Davie!" she whispered loudly.  "I admire you for what you've done for Willie."

"Then why does everybody try to make something out of it?" David felt the rush of blood to his face.  "Is it so terrible for me to care about whether or not my friend dies?"

"Don't be so touchy."

"Touchy?  What if everybody kept hinting and whispering that you were a lesbian?  How would that make you feel?  Maybe touchy?"

She gazed at him with soft brown eyes.  David remembered Alicia appearing in his tent last night, then vanishing again.  He didn't know what he was talking about now.

"Am I black, Davie?"

"What?"  Now he was confused.  He saw no hostility in her eyes.  He groped through his recollection of how this conversation had started.  He could not follow the thread.

"Do you think I'm black?"

David had never really thought about it.  He looked at her light brown, satin face, her delicate lips, her petite pointy nose with its precisely sculpted, oval nostrils.  "Why are you asking me that?"

"You have to answer."

"I don't know.  Sort of a little black.  That sounds stupid."

"Some of the black kids treat me like I'm white.  And most of the white kids treat me like I'm black."

"So you're kind of caught in the middle."

"No.  I'm not caught at all.  It's everybody else that's caught."

"I don't follow you."

"There's only one reason why anybody has to decide whether I'm black or white, and that's so they can decide if they should treat me like a real person or not.  But I already know I'm a real person.  I have to live every day with people who are caught in their own traps.  They're the one's who have to ask themselves if I'm one of their own kind."

"So where did all this stuff come from all of a sudden?"

Alicia paused, watching Willie as he slept.  "First of all...This is embarrassing."

"What?"

"I kind of wanted to know if Willie had a girl friend, because...well, because I really like him...a lot."

David felt the jolt of suddenly understanding the obvious. Somehow the possibility that Alicia liked Willie had escaped his consideration.

"And," she continued, "...I wondered if Willie thought of me as a...real person." She took David's hand. "I know you do. And I feel really safe and comfortable with you...or I guess I wouldn't be talking about this."

"If you're asking me if Willie wants to go with you, I guess I don't know. But he's not a bigot."

"Then you got all huffy about why I was asking about him. The only reason anybody has to call me names is if they want to prove that it's okay to treat me like dirt."

"I just misunderstood what you were saying." David squirmed as the subject of the conversation seemed to swing back to him.

"Well, maybe you did," she replied, "but, all the same, you're too smart to wonder whether or not to treat yourself like dirt."

David's fatigued mind puzzled at his sense of relief. Whatever it was that Alicia was trying to tell him seemed vaguely reassuring. He felt a subliminal joy that Alicia was interested in Willie. And it was comforting, in all the chaos, to have Alicia nearby, confiding in him. He kissed her hand.

Alicia stood. "Good night, Davie." She leaned down and pressed her cheek against his.


Jeffrey Horn was breathing sixty times a minute, the best he could estimate. The pain in his right chest was unrelenting. He had been walking in the dark for nearly two hours when he reached the now familiar intersection of the Tonto Trail with the wider Plateau Point Trail.

His left hand pressed a cellophane cigarette wrapper against the wound in his chest. It still leaked air and blood when he breathed. The mere act of breathing exhausted him. The undulating slopes of the Tonto required enormous effort. He wondered if he could make the climb out of the Canyon. Would it make more sense just to wait at the ranger station and surrender?

Rapid breathing had dried his mouth, and his water bottles were empty. He turned onto the wider trail and headed south, toward Indian Garden.

## BRIGHT ANGEL

As the sky outside "Mother Cave" became light, Jay Vesco approached the mouth. The sky is finally blue, he thought. He looked down to the rocks south of him, and saw that the others were gone. Anger swelled. *They didn't even bring up any water.* When Laura and that homo, Davie, had not returned, he decided to sleep for a while. He had been certain they would wake him up when they got back. When he had finally awakened to find it dark, he decided he may as well just sleep through the night.

Now he could see their plan to leave him as bait for the killer. He could see through that. With daylight, he decided to climb down and make a run for Indian Garden and then out of the Canyon. *They can all go to hell. And carrying Willie, that's really stupid. He's going to die anyway.* It was only for Laura's benefit he risked his life going so slow. Now the ungrateful bitch sneaks away. *Well, fuck her. Fuck them all.*

Feet first, he eased his way out of "Mother Cave" and groped with his foot for the first step. A cold, sickening feeling rose up from his groin. He closed his eyes, only to see Willie's purple jacket extend its arms and soar in the warm updraft.


Jeffrey Horn lost the race to be out of the Canyon by dawn. He looked to the sky above the Rim. It appeared cloudless as it grew lighter. In clear weather, the deep snow above would make his task of evasion a more serious challenge.

For the moment he satisfied himself with small victories. He had successfully passed Indian Garden during the night. There had been lights on and movement visible through the windows of the ranger station. He had considered stopping, surrendering. It was shame, more than fear that had dissuaded him. He needed help, but knew he was undeserving of it. He had decided to continue.   He had been able to slip by, undetected, despite his noisy breathing.   He had filled his water bottles at the spigot below the latrine, unobserved.

The massive cliff of the Redwall had dominated his psyche for a week.  It had become an even greater burden on his mind since the girl had stabbed him with the deer antler.  He had pushed his endurance, gasping for air with every agonizing step up the brutal switchbacks.  The map had labeled it "Jacob's Ladder."  It had felt as though each step drew him one step closer to meeting his maker, an encounter that he assumed would not go well.

Although disappointed at climbing only part way up the Canyon wall by dawn, Horn was satisfied to have come so far. He now rested on a bench at Three Mile Resthouse, lamenting the passing of night, the arrival of day.

He looked up toward the snow covered Rim.  Deep snow. Crampons would probably be necessary, he thought, to prevent him from slipping off the upper trails.  With a pocket knife in hand, he went to a stunted juniper and sliced off several lower branches, each as thick as his thumb.  Returning with them to the rest house, he trimmed them into foot long segments, eight of them, with two-inch side branches sharpened to points.  From the stolen backpack, he brought out two lashing straps made of one inch nylon webbing, with a plastic buckle at one end of each strap.  He arranged four of the juniper segments so that the spikes angled in the same direction, then strapped them to the bottom of his right boot.  Bending to reach his boots increased his chest pain and made breathing more difficult.

The strap would be more useful in the future if he did not cut it, but the danger of tripping over a dangling strap while traversing an icy canyon trail, outweighed the value of a longer strap.  He cut the strap, leaving seven inches beyond the buckle, enough to grasp and tighten his jury-rigged crampons.  Horn removed the short strap and used it to measure the second strap, which he cut to the same length.  He put the straps and juniper branches into his pack.

Before starting up the Supai, Horn looked back toward Indian Garden.  Movement!  Seven hundred feet below, a group of people were starting up the trail.  About a half-dozen, he guessed.

He slipped his arms into the pack straps and headed up the trail. The rest had slowed his rapid breathing slightly. The pain was worse.


Bill Gluzack was not sure why he had decided to join the rangers stomping down the Canyon through deep snow. Ranger Rantoon had already assembled two other rangers to take down, when Gluzack added himself to the group. Somebody else can wrestle with the phone calls today. He needed to get a handle on what was going on below the rim.

Part of his apprehension stemmed from the repair of the phone line to Indian Garden. He had let it ring for ten minutes this morning without an answer. With both Maria and Mandi down there, someone should have answered. Adding to his concern was the failure of the Thurman party to climb out yesterday. With a killer roaming the Canyon, Gluzack could not comfort himself with any of the more benign explanations of these puzzles. His head told him to be patient. His gut told him to climb down with a gun. Even though he would have a helicopter crew searching in two hours, he felt compelled to hike down.

The storm had ended, leaving the Rim in two and a half feet of snow under a clear sky. The temperature hung in the low twenties. Snow and ice, Gluzack thought, would probably extend well into the Coconino. All four of the men walked with instep crampons strapped to their boots. Jason Rantoon led; Gluzack walked in the rear. He had expected to reach the Coconino by now, but the snow at the top was deeper and more treacherous than he had ever seen. This alone would have provided justification for any hiking party to turn back in their attempt to climb out. But he had found no trace of footsteps. He thought he could see movement below, but it was difficult to be sure.


Jay moved confidently up Bright Angel Trail above Indian Garden. The rhythmic pounding of his feet on hardpack trail exhilarated him, as he sped to catch up with the others. He had paused at the campground only long enough to drink directly from the water spigot. He would now maintain his present pace until he caught them. He occasionally saw movement high above, at the base of the Redwall.

He thought about the man with the gun. He envisioned holding his own gun to the man's head. "Lick my boots," he would say, "or I'll splatter your fucking brains on the dirt." And then he pictured with satisfaction the look of surprise on the man's face when he shot him anyway.


David tightened the straps of his instep crampons.

"How do these go, Davie," Alicia asked.

"I'll get it," he said. David attached the crampons to Alicia's boots. Alicia's hand touched his own. David looked up and saw tenderness.

"You're not mad at me, are you?" Alicia asked in a whisper.

"What for?" David was lost.

"You know, in the tent."

"I figured you just didn't want to be alone." He remembered again awakening to find her in the tent two nights ago.

She smiled. "That's true. When Laura went to Jay's tent, I got kind of scared."

"I wasn't mad," David said.

"But I meant the night down at the rapids," she clarified. David felt his ears flush. He wasn't sure exactly what happened that night. Did she mean because she left, he wondered, or because of something she did before she left? "What was I supposed to be mad about?" he asked.

"You weren't mad?"

"No. Should I have been?" he asked. This was not clearing up the troublesome questions he had wrestled with for three days. He couldn't think of a way to ask her how and where she had touched him that night. Or if she had touched him.

"David," Maria called from the far end of Willie's litter, "catch." She gently tossed a pair of crampons. "Tie them to those two corners, like this."

David looked at the front corners of the litter, where Maria had strapped on crampons. He did the same on the rear.

"These will keep the stretcher right where we put it down," she said.

"Does the trail get worse, higher up?" Laura asked.

"The snow gets deep, but if you watch your step, you shouldn't have any problem."

During the night, David had watched a second liter bag of fluid run into Willie's IV. Because of the freezing temperature on the Rim, and because of the difficulty of managing the IV during the climb out, Maria removed the IV before they left the ranger station. To protect the foot that extended beyond the sleeping bag, David had wrapped the bottom of the splint with Willie's purple, nylon jacket.

As he prepared to continue the exhausting climb with the stretcher, David remembered the two segments of his lashing straps that he had found at Three Mile Resthouse. He had mentioned this to Maria. Since then, it seemed to him that she had been more worried and more alert.

To David, the idea of a chase or a gunfight on the icy trails was nothing short of insanity. Even without bullets sailing back and forth, a simple slip could be fatal.

With the crampons in place, David hefted his corner of the litter and started up the trail again. Ranger Sanchez walked with Laura, hauling the long basket behind them. David and Alicia carried the rear. Even seeing the sun for the first time in a week could not drive away the cold that became more chilling as they ascended the Coconino.


Every step tore at SSgt. Horn's body. Resting brought little relief. The deeper he breathed, the more severe was the pain in his chest. His thighs ached for more oxygen. He could not slow down. The hikers below him were gaining. He was fairly certain that they were the kids from the campsite, accompanied by a ranger. They carried a stretcher. *Willie Thurman got help after all.*

He gained some small satisfaction from the effectiveness of his improvised, juniper crampons. Their spikes bit into the crust, but the single strap holding each set of twigs required constant tightening to prevent the buckle from rotating. Once already, he had tripped on the trailing strap, landing on his right side and starting the bleeding again from his chest wound. The pain had been sufficient to remind him to check the straps frequently.

Doubt swept into his mind. He was smothering. He breathed as rapidly and as deeply as he could, yet he was unable to meet the demands of his muscles. His chest felt ready to burst. His mind dulled from the exhaustion and pain and suffocation. He might not be able to reach the Rim.

Just one more switchback, he thought. Think of only one at a time. No, that's too far. Think of only one step. *Take one step.   Take one step.* "Take...one... step." *Stop...talking. Just...breathe. One step. One step.*

The pain in his chest gnawed at his determination to go on. *One...step. In the white snow he sees the camo covered face looking at him. But now it seems to be grimly smiling back at him, pleased with this agonal drama.* "It's just a game." *One step. Just a game. Just a game.*

Horn looked up, the white edges of the switchbacked trail bobbing as he panted. Movement. He saw movement above. *One step. Rangers. Four rangers coming down.* The steep slope of a switchback halted his progress. *One step.* No, he could not step up.

*It's over. The game is over.* He could not step. He could not hide. He could not fight. He could not even breathe. Staff Sergeant Jeffrey Horn stood gasping for air.

"That's him," a voice yelled from above.

"Freeze!" he heard from below.

Horn looked down. Twenty feet below stood the ranger he had shot. It seemed like weeks ago. Now, she held him again in the sights of her gun.

Four rangers were rushing down from the trail terrace above him. The last one stopped above and leveled a gun at him. Horn's legs quivered. He could hardly stand on the twist of the trail. Three men approached him, guns drawn. He remembered his own gun, tucked in his belt. It was no longer a consideration. He would surrender, because he could do nothing else. He was dying of suffocation. He was dying of pain.

Horn decided to sit down. He could stand no longer. He took one small step down. *It's not right.* He realized, in a fleeting second of understanding, that the same troublesome lashing strap had now tripped him again.

He fell from the icy trail. Jagged rocks gashed his shoulder. Then his leg. The world rushed past. He struck the flat of the trail below with his right arm. The forearm broke at the wrist with an audible snap and excruciating pain. For a second, he saw the ranger he had shot before. He slid from the trail floating in the air for a half second. A rock jabbed his back. More pain. For only a moment, he thought of his mother dying in a car wreck.

With a hollow thud, he landed on his back at the edge of the trail, his legs dangling over. There, through the haze of agony he recognized the tall skinny kid who had given him the water bottle. The boy reached for him. Horn saw concern on the boy's face. Horn toppled over the ice covered lip. He slid momentarily over abrasive scree, then cleared the slope, falling. As he struck the trail below, his right leg shattered. He crashed to his back and stopped. He was surprised that, above all the pain, he felt still more from his leg.

As his mind blurred, he became aware of the bigger boy, the one he had almost shot at the campsite. The boy held a huge rock in his hands, lifting it into the startling blue sky. *It's just a game.*


Jay Vesco felt a familiar rush of victory as he lifted the hundred pound slab of cream colored sandstone above his head. With all the power of his arms and torso, he slammed the rock onto the head of the man lying on the trail. It crushed.

"Yes!" Jay shouted, thrusting his arms into the air.

## COLUMBIA

"It's really strange," Willie said, "to have Laura treating me like her twin brother instead of a piece of shit." He paged through a dog-eared copy of Playboy magazine. "Yesterday she actually asked me what CD I wanted to listen to. I had to mark that on the calendar. Oh, Jeeze!" Willie's braces flashed between his lips as he folded back a page and showed it to David.

"Boobs are too big," David commented.

"And last night she asked my opinion about which color blouse I thought she looked better in."

"What's wrong with that?"

"Nothing. I guess there's a first time for everything." Willie continued to page through the magazine. "You know, Davie, some of these are really gross. Like this one." He showed the page.

"She needs some clothes," David offered, adjusting his blue retainer.

"Not clothes; just like the corner of a satin bed sheet or something."

"Davie," Mrs. Cadranel's voice called through the closed bedroom door, "it's getting late."

Willie rolled up the mattress edge and buried the magazine.

"Okay, Mom," David answered, "good night."
Footsteps receded from the door. Willie looked at David, then both of them laughed.

"You're such a wuz, Willie."

"Hey, what did you throw that out for?" Willie grabbed his crutches and swung his legs off the bed. He hopped over to David's waste basket and retrieved a ten week old copy of the Columbia Missourian newspaper.

"I was tired of puking every time I saw it," David said.

"Even if it is only the 'Manurean', at least save my picture," Willie suggested.

David looked at the familiar headline: HIGH SCHOOL QB STOPS SERIAL KILLER. Beside the flattering portrait of Jay was the photo that Willie had taken at Hermit Rapids, showing Jeffrey Horn kneeling by the water.

"Or do you just want to forget about Horn?" Willie asked.

"It's not Horn. It's Jay I want to forget about."

"Yeah, I guess Laura was the one who actually stopped him, when you think about it," Willie speculated.

Willie just didn't get it, David thought. He had not discussed the circumstances surrounding Willie's fall. When Willie had first been awake enough to talk about the whole ordeal, it had been around the time of the funeral for Mr. Thurman. Willie didn't even learn of his father's death until the day before the funeral. In his daily visits to the hospital, David had not broached his suspicions about Jay, because he had assumed that Willie was intentionally avoiding the subject. If Willie really did not remember what had happened, maybe he should leave it that way.

"Willie, what do you remember about the day you fell?"

"Not a lot. I remember the campsite flooded in the morning. Dad hurt his hand on the Agave in Monument Creek. The last thing I remember is Dad ordering me to go fill the water bottles."

"You don't remember the fall?"

"I don't even remember what the place looks like. After that, I have sort of fuzzy memories, like Ezra," he pointed to the rust stained rabbit on the pillow, "and you telling me to pee in a towel," he laughed, "and a helicopter. That's about it. What did I miss?"

"It's just hard to imagine you getting so close to the edge of the waterfall that you could fall off."

"I hiked down Hermit gorge in the dark."

"That's true."

"I knew my dad wouldn't believe it. That's why I took the picture that you threw out."

"I didn't throw it out. Well, what I mean is I was throwing out all that bullshit Jay told the reporter. I guess I do want your picture."

"My dad never did know that I went down there."

"If he had found out, you'd probably have been grounded for a month. But you know you went down there. Of course, you ended up grounded for two and a half months instead." David could not decide if he should stir up the business about Jay, but Willie needed to know.

"Willie, has Jay talked to you since you came home?"

"Not much. He just looks at me kind of funny. Actually, he has passed up a few opportunities to get in some digs. Why all the questions about Jay and when I fell?"

David hesitated. "Jay scares the crap out of me. He scared me more than Horn. I'd just steer clear of him."

Willie was silent. He seemed to wait for a more satisfying explanation.

"How's it going with you and Alicia," David asked, interested only in getting off the subject of Jay.

"Great. She's really cool."

"Your mom doesn't give you any grief about her?"

"Mom's always liked her," Willie answered. "It was Dad that couldn't deal with her skin color." Sadness came over his face for a moment, then Willie smiled. "You know, it's funny, that night down by the rapids."

David felt awkward. "Yeah?"

"When we woke up doing the touchy feelies," Willie chuckled, "I had this sudden fear that we'd done some, you know, really strange things during the night."

David could only sit and listen. He could feel his ears turning red.

"Well, let me just say that I was mighty relieved last week when Alicia told me she left the tent just before dawn."

David's entire body relaxed. That hadn't been Willie in the middle of the night. And since Willie and Alicia were now going together, he couldn't see any reason to muck it up.

"How about some sleep?" David said. David unrolled the two sleeping bags onto the floor, unzipping Willie's. Willie hopped over to the bag, stripped off his clothes and scooted into the bag. David leaned over to zip Willie's bag.

"I can get it," Willie said, with some irritation. "It's not like I'm a cripple."

David undressed and climbed into his own sleeping bag. He climbed back out, turned off the light and returned to his bag.

"Good night, Willie."

"Good night."

David realized that Willie's desperate need had fused an indelible bond. He remembered, during those awful days, the reassuring sigh of Willie's breathing. It had imprinted itself so deeply into his awareness that David now slept soundly only on the weekend nights when Willie stayed over. David recalled the weeknights, alone, awakening frequently, afraid of the silence. He would wander downstairs to sit beside the shelves of books in his living room.

David watched Willie sleep in the dappled light that filtered through the window curtain. He knew that Willie would never understand how much David had invested of himself, and how irreversible that was. Willie, he acknowledged, had become a part of his soul. He closed his eyes, knowing tonight he would sleep well.

## THE END

www.ingramcontent.com/pod-product-compliance
Lightning Source LLC
Chambersburg PA
CBHW030514260626
47157CB00005B/1739